# Tanaki on the Shore

# TANAKI
## ON THE SHORE

A NOVEL BY
# BILL SMITH

PORTAL PRESS
WASHINGTON, D.C.

Published in the United States of America


"Tankas XII and XV by Yokiko Asano, translated by Kenneth Rexroth in ONE HUNDRED POEMS FROM THE JAPANESE copyright © 1976 by Kenneth Rexroth. Reprinted by permission of New Directions Publishing Corp. SALES TERRITORY: U.S. Canadian rights only."


Library of Congress Control Number: 2005904827
ISBN 13: 978-1-933454-00-9
ISBN 10: 1-933454-00-8


Portal Press
1327 Irving Street, N.E.
Washington, D.C. 20017
www.theportalpress.com

*The author gratefully acknowledges Lisa Mick and the Portal Press staff for invaluable assistance in editing this novel.*

This book is dedicated to
everyone working to save the Chesapeake

# TANAKI on the SHORE

*A Few Years Back*

# 1

# *Tanaki*

The Honda slowed as David Tanaki pressed the brake pedal, carefully guiding the sedan between booths, easing it under the arching toll gate that stood like a *torii* before the bay. He tossed four quarters into the gaping metal basket with a loud jangle, the light went to green, and the fragile wooden barrier lifted on the wetlands of Maryland's eastern shore. Of course he had known he'd be crossing the bridge—it was in the very thorough directions Guy Folker faxed from the research station a month earlier—but nothing had prepared him for the spectacle that surrounded him as he clipped up the approach ramp and climbed the floating band of concrete toward the steel supports ahead, where the bridge straightens out before resuming its elegant curve on the descent toward Kent Island six miles away. It was near ten o'clock on an April morning, and the waters of the bay reflected the clean, pure spring light with a brilliance that was blinding. He stole brief glances to his right, careful to obey signs instructing STAY IN LANE or MAINTAIN SPEED, trying to get a better look down the length of the bay toward the estuary's mouth, but the interstices in the crash barrier afforded only a broken view of the rippled and glittering surface. He wanted to stop the car and look over the rail, but block letters warning STAY IN VEHICLE and NO PEDESTRIANS spoke to him with an authority he wouldn't question. Somewhere up around the central span, four-hundred feet over the bay's waters, where giant, steel cables swing like hawsers left behind by a doomed race of Titanic sailors, Tanaki began to think of Mrs. Scofield. Funny, he hadn't thought about it for years. The annual ritual, a summer vacation on the Upper Peninsula with Tom's family. But now he remembered it all clearly. The tense silence beginning an hour from the Straits, where they passed the boat repair shop. Tom's father knocking himself out to maintain a patter of pleasant conversation, hoping to distract his wife from her fears. The way sweat would bead up on her forehead when the bridge came into view, her frantic refusals to go another inch—please let me out here, I'll walk back, you go on—saying crazy things, it all ending with her crawling onto the floor in back until solid ground was again under the wheels. Tanaki remembered how odd it felt to have Tom's mother, who made egg salad sandwiches just the way he liked them when he visited, lying across his tennis shoes, hands covering a face grown red from holding her breath. And the time she begged Tom's father to lock her in the trunk for the crossing, emerging disheveled, hair mussed and dress askew, one shoe still in the trunk when they pulled over at the Dairy Queen on the other side. Looking back now, Mrs. Scofield didn't seem so strange. After all, Tanaki thought, there was no way to prove that the bridge really connected the two shores, or that the two shores existed once he motored onto the bridge, or that the world he encountered on the other side would be the same one he left behind. "People spend their lives looking for bridges . . . or fleeing them," he thought, as he began the descent toward Kent Island, the Honda—a mere seventeen-hundred pounds of metal, plastic and rubber—whirring across so many thousands of tons of substance like a toy. Glancing to the north he noted herring gulls . . . *larus argentatus*, he thought . . . wheeling aloft off the bridge's railing. Finally the bridge devolved onto the causeway that skimmed over the bay's surface for the remaining half-mile to the Eastern Shore.

Ugly chain stores lined the highway on the other side of the bridge. Their dumb, stolid inertia dampened Tanaki's spirits, leaving him mute and heavy. But after a couple of miles the modern development thinned out; he passed a fishing supplies store with a blue marlin sign and other establishments with names like *The Dunes Cafe* and *Sea Crest Hardware*; he was now in water's realm. After following the ramp up the embankment, motoring southward into the Delmarva peninsula, he took note of flooded forest off the roadway, intercut with narrow creeks, open marsh and spreading coves. Further on he cruised past miles of alluvial fields, some covered with a soft down of new wheat, others bare or in stubble; and lonely farmhouses standing in vast spaces, utterly exposed except for a few shade trees and out-buildings; and in the distance hazy stands of low forest.

Folker's directions were indeed thorough. Tanaki had looked them over before setting out, had noted the large star representing the Chesapeake Wetlands Research Center on the accompanying map, but hadn't referred to them since leaving Michigan. A fact not in itself remarkable, the principal highways between the upper Midwest and the Mid-Atlantic well-marked and straightforward; but now, as he approached the final leg of his journey, when he would leave the traffic on the main highway and follow back roads to the research station; now, when it would be the most natural thing in the world to reach into the glovebox and remove the shiny rolled FAX paper, he declined to do so. Instead, he motored steadily onto the low bridge crossing the ample width of the Choptank River, bisected the commercial jetsam lining the highway as it skirted Cambridge, and turned right at the Food Lion.

Without thinking about it he was deciding against going to the research station, where Guy Folker and company were expecting his arrival that afternoon. Not that he felt any aversion toward the Center's staff. He simply knew that his first encounter with the bay should be an intimate affair, something between him and Nature. He'd been studying the bay's ecosystems for months in preparation for the fellowship, and the estuary had taken on a personality of its own for him. He was also anxious to see if tundra swans might still be in the area, though surely the bulk of the migrants had winged northward at least a month earlier. So he made his way to the Blackwater Wildlife Refuge, oblivious to park-service-brown signs indicating directions to the sprawling wetlands.

Turning into the preserve, he slowed the Honda to a crawl. He slipped the requisite five dollars into the metal kiosk that stood beside the drive and proceeded onto the loop road, a scar of dry earth raised out of the marshes. Cruising slowly with an arm hanging out the window, stopping at intervals to peer over the still, liquid expanses, he saw no sign of migratory waterfowl, but began to feel an unmistakable sense of peace.

After leaving the refuge he called Folker to let him know he was in the area but wouldn't make it to the station before five as planned. He maundered down the peninsula, eventually arching over a steep bridge to Hooper Island, a thin strip of land separated from the mainland at its northern end by only a few feet of bay. Near the island's southern tip he pulled off the road to observe two swans feeding in the shallows. He walked onto the intertidal flat that sponged under his steps and felt a breeze coming off the water. The swans weren't migratory tundras but nonindigenous mutes, considered a "nuisance species" by some folks around the bay, but he was happy to have found them anyway. Shortly an impatient man with New York plates pulled off the road. He stepped onto the flat long enough to take a quick look at the graceful animals, headed back to his car with a disappointed "trash birds"—then rushed off to some unimaginable destination.

In the wake of the New Yorker's departure Tanaki stood in a silence broken only by the slap of a desultory tide against the mud flat, watching the swans, who were now drifting into a sun that was rapidly declining toward the western shore. He wanted to call out to the birds, beckon them back, but with a twinge in the solar plexus he resigned himself to the improbability of such an inter-species communication. The sun cast a pale golden glow across the water and shore and the quiet of the place engulfed him. He became aware, in what seemed a novel manner, that his feet were planted in the earth, that his eyes perceived the falling sun and rippling water, that his skin felt the moist breeze. Responding to a sudden urge he dropped into a squatting position and listened intently. There were gulls squawking in the distance; their rarefied cries seemed to whisper something.

His eyes sought out the swans. They were well into the offing, elegant whitenesses against the green of the water. As he watched them move towards the depths he reflected that they'd no doubt spent their entire lives around the estuary, the Chesapeake's mute population being non-migratory. How different, he thought, than his own peripatetic existence—the life of a wandering scholar, seeking his permanent place in the world. They seemed so much a part of the bay, of its land and seascapes, while he'd just be passing through, adding another block of understanding in his chosen field and another credential to his resume. Yet something felt so true about being here, he felt such kinship with these two swans, indeed with everything he perceived around him, that he couldn't help but think that right here at the bay he might find something like home.

A stiffening in his knee joints forced him up. He held each leg off the ground and agitated it, shaking out the kinks. The quickening breeze against his torso seemed to push him along, but to where? The swans had now drifted so far away he could hardly make them out.

He made his way back to the arching bridge. Hooper Island seemed deserted in spite of sea-beaten bungalows that stood in long, rectangular yards along narrow lanes that ran to the bay, and workboats strung along docks that branched like coral reefs into the Honga River. The only sign of life was a road crew operating a backhoe near the northern end. Tanaki waited in the forlorn afternoon while the scoop was maneuvered out of his lane.

He stopped for gas at the only service station since Cambridge, not a service station really, but a boat shop with a couple old pumps out front and a general store inside. A white-haired local took payment while a pair of aging collies milled blindly around the little market.

He arrived at Folker's house late in the day. Darkness was investing the quiet neighborhood of stately colonials when he eased the Honda around a new Jaguar parked in the drive. Two girls and a boy of grade school age greeted him shyly as he emerged from the car, and offered to help with his bags. The four of them made their way clumsily to the front door, where Miriam Folker introduced herself and let a hungry Tanaki know that dinner was ready. Guy Folker showed him to a room down a side hallway where he'd stay until he found a place of his own.

After dinner the children rushed off to their entertainments while the adults sipped coffee around the dining room table.

"Guy tells me you're a migration specialist," Miriam said. "You know I do some painting—I especially like shorebirds. Are there any particular species you work with?"

"Not really," he said. "If it moves, it interests me. And you know everything, at least every *living* thing, moves. Because of the research opportunities I've had so far, I've seen more of birds than anything else." Then glancing toward Guy he added, "but I'm excited about working on some marine species while I'm here."

"You couldn't find a better place," Guy said, pulling a pipe from his jacket. "The largest bay in the continental U.S., after all."

"With a watershed running up to New York and out to West Virginia," Tanaki responded in a voice alive with wonder. "And a migration-shed that's even more extensive." Then, suddenly remembering Miriam, "Miriam, I guess this may not have anything to do with painting."

"Maybe not. But I find it fascinating anyway. Especially this idea of a migration-shed."

"Imagine geese and swans migrating back and forth from their summer breeding grounds above the Arctic Circle," Tanaki said. "I was up there last year. Then a bunch of summer-resident birds that winter in South America. Or Monarch butterflies coming in huge swarms from Mexico. As for the fish, some of them call the entire Atlantic home. Tell you the truth, it's almost scary what we're trying to do, make sense of all this phenomena."

"I hope my migration man's not saying he's got the jitters," Folker put in, settling back in his chair.

"I didn't say I'm not up to it," Tanaki said. "But there are so many ways you can go wrong, with so much data in constant flux." He glanced at Miriam, finding reassurance in her eyes, then turned again to Guy. "Sometimes I almost envy those lab researchers. You know, it would be so much easier if we could put the whole estuary in a test tube, control all the inputs and outputs, all the variables."

"If pigs had wings . . ." Folker replied.

"I'd probably be studying them," Tanaki said with a laugh that took in both the Folkers. "But seriously," he continued, "I've come to believe it's the integrity of your system that counts. That's where the order comes in. Out there it's just, you know, chaos. But I don't mean that in a bad way."

Folker was occupied stuffing his pipe.

"Sounds like painting," Miriam said.

There was a pause, then Tanaki replied, "I would have never thought of that."

"But it's true. And isn't it that challenge—bringing meaning to chaos—that keeps it interesting?"

"I do enjoy the challenge."

"Well," Folker said, drawing on his pipe, "I like a man who rises to a struggle. Faint hearts never won fair maidens, as they say. But listen, why don't we step out onto the porch. I'm sure Miriam, speaking of fair maidens, would like to show you her watercolors."

They spent the evening on a screened porch, reviewing Miriam's artistic efforts—gulls and beached sailboats—before slipping into a discussion of the local real estate market, the ever-changing weather patterns of the shore, and odd scraps from news of the day. With his steady gaze and relaxed demeanor Folker came across as professorial, settled into a wicker armchair, puffing leisurely on his pipe. Miriam was thoughtful and quite lovely. But Tanaki felt an odd disquiet in their presence, as if some unseen force were operating on the household, threatening to bring him as well within its grip. He was relieved when they excused themselves to put the children to bed; it gave him a pretext to turn in himself. He retired to his room where he lay enjoying a view of pines and stars before fading into an uneasy sleep.

## 2

# *The Bluebird*

"Who's there?"

The voice was faint but direct.

"David Tanaki," he replied, standing on the porch of the three-story Victorian that stood behind two great magnolias, forcing his voice through a door encrusted with dark paint scored by vertical fissures. The door creaked and the musty odor of a house kept by the elderly wafted onto the porch, filling his nostrils, getting into his hair, his eyes, his shoes. Straining to see into the dimness, he perceived a shadowy figure drifting back-ward into the hallway without discernable movement of limbs, as he imagined a ghost might move. When his eyes adjusted he made out a woman, probably pushing ninety, standing beside an antique cabinet the doors of which were alive with swirling fish and other marine motifs. The outline of a staircase emerged from the left side of the foyer. Still there was something about the woman's appearance—perhaps it was the faded dress, or the way her hair seemed to float above her head—that heightened the wraith-like quality he'd sensed in her movements.

"You've come about the room?" she inquired, her accented voice rising in a wan glissando.

"Yes . . . I'm beginning a fellowship at the research station down in Benton," Tanaki began; but he broke off his remark, sensing that the details of his life held little interest for his prospective landlady. She was already moving toward the bottom of the staircase, and with a feeble hand drew a large key ring from the pocket of her housedress. She took hold of the bannister, placed a foot on the first step, and climbed without a word until reaching a capacious landing on the second floor. She turned and presented the keys to Tanaki, weakly gesturing to one side.

"This is the apartment," she said formally, "examine it carefully."

Tanaki stepped aside to let her pass. She descended the staircase with the same gliding fatigue with which she'd ascended it. He looked around the landing. Like the foyer, it was furnished with several objects of apparent antiquity—a dark, ornate sideboard, a rudely carved cigar store Indian, a weathered sailor's trunk. He placed the key in the lock and stepped inside, his footsteps echoing on the hardwood floor. The apartment consisted of a living room of ample dimensions with two windows facing the magnolias, a galley kitchen with a small breakfast room, and a bedroom facing the backyard. After walking slowly through each of the rooms, he stood in the living room assessing what sort of feeling the place gave him. His career had involved many a change of residence over the past twelve years, and he'd determined that his first impression was normally the best indicator of whether a place would work out or not. He suspected this had something to do with the same kind of faculty that was thought to help birds on their first migration know when they've reached the right place. Possessed of an innate impression of how a habitat should feel, look, and smell, the nature of the terrain and flora, the quality of the sunlight, they orient themselves in the proper direction and stop when they reach a site that corresponds to their inner Shangri-la. Tanaki followed the same principle—the only trick was to relax enough to let his instincts take over.

He didn't know what to make of the landlady; she, like the artifacts in the hallway, lent the place the aura of an earlier century. But these factors didn't come to the fore as he stood in the empty room making his decision. He was instead struck by a certain austerity about the apartment that he found agreeable. He even considered leaving the rooms largely unfurnished to draw attention to the wood floors and the oyster-shell white walls. The view out the windows would provide relief in the waxy greenness of the magnolia leaves. Making up his mind at once, he moved briskly to the door and descended the stairs to tell the landlady he was ready to sign the lease.

As he passed through the dilapidated gate onto Talbot Street, he was aware of a raw, misty drizzle against his face. It reminded him, along with the overcast sky and the sense of antiquity surrounding his new residence, of the Netherlands, where he'd spent a couple of years doing doctoral research. And as he turned the corner at an eighteenth-century church with a rose window over the entrance, his thoughts devolved, in spite of himself, upon the Bluebird.

They met for the first time in a cafe in a coastal town where folks rode right out to the beach in their automobiles. He'd been in Europe only a few weeks and she was a Belgian who'd studied at the Sorbonne and in Spain and Hamburg. She told him later that she'd known right away he was a "navigationist," meaning his abiding interest was in getting to the bottom of Perdecci's astonishing work.

Tanaki had come with Pannenburg, his academic sponsor and mentor, for the express purpose of meeting several colleagues, the Bluebird among them. Pannenburg ran a research station situated at the tip of one of the headlands that jut into the North Sea, a remote, windswept place among dunes and dune grasses, ideal for spotting the migrating flocks that collect in large numbers on the shores before making their crossings *en masse*. A bear of a man, with battleship-gray hair falling loosely onto a bluff forehead, Pannenburg had a reputation for sound science and creative thinking. For some reason he'd taken Tanaki under his wing from the start; the two of them were soon working as if they'd been collaborating for years.

The cafe was right off the beach, and from where Tanaki sat he could see iridescent glintings of moonlight illuminating the surf in the distance. The Bluebird arrived with Dietrich Moeller, one of the reigning demigods of the migration field. Moeller was in charge of a European-wide banding project that had been initiated with great fanfare in the fifties. Impeccably tailored, with thin dark hair combed back from a receding hairline, he'd been a friend of Pannenberg's since they studied under Perdecci years before.

He introduced the Bluebird as his assistant. The connection of the young biologist Euler wasn't spelled out, and Tanaki didn't ask.

Pannenburg opened the conversation by praising Tanaki effusively.

"Yes, I have high hopes for this fellow," he said. "He's a man to watch."

"Really . . ." an embarrassed Tanaki protested.

"You hear that Ani, I hope you're watching him," Moeller said with a sly wink. "That is unless you'd rather watch Heinz."

"Maybe I'll watch them both," she countered deftly, "or focus on my own career, if you don't mind."

"Why not," Pannenburg put in. "She's nicer to watch than Heinz or David. And isn't her talent second to none?"

"Of course," Moeller replied, "That's precisely why I hired her. In fact, she's the most capable student I've ever had." Seemingly disconcerted by this open praise of his assistant, Moeller added more quietly, "She knows I'm only teasing."

"Nothing wrong with a little levity, I always say," Pannenburg added. "Now, as for Heinz, well . . ."

"If you're going to start picking on me . . ." Euler began.

"Now, now," Pannenburg cajoled. "In fact, I was just predicting the other day that your rise will be nothing short of meteoric. Ask Dietrich. But first, why don't you see if you can get that waitress's attention and get us some food, more beer . . ."

After a discussion of academic appointments—Moeller: "Really, Gunther, can you believe they're giving the Heidelberg post to Fanon? Remember how we used to call him Fussy-pants?"—the conversation turned to the research that consumed most of their waking lives. Those were tremendously heady days in migration studies, and conversations between migration biologists could flame into a passion normally reserved for questions of political moment or affairs of the heart. Everyone was working in the wake of Perdecci, scrambling to make sense of his paradigm-shattering experiments of the sixties, and it seemed new worlds were always on the verge of opening up—though never clearly perceptible.

Tanaki watched Pannenburg and Moeller, two shaggy-maned old lions, heatedly argue the possibility that birds use the earth's magnetic field to orient themselves, interjecting no more than a clarifying question, reluctant to enter the fray. But Euler and the Bluebird evinced no such reticence, and bantered freely with their older colleagues.

During the course of the evening Tanaki became interested in Moeller's young assistant, though at first he hadn't found her remarkable. She was of medium height, her tawny hair long and straight. If there was anything that distinguished her appearance it was the intelligence of her expression. But it was her style of argument, more than anything, which drew Tanaki to her. Instead of taking on a point directly, she'd strike obliquely with a remark that, while not seeming to contradict Pannenburg or Moeller, subverted the entire train of thought in some insidious way. In fact, he conjectured, the older guys probably thought she was agreeing with them most of the time. But on one occasion she stopped the discussion short by responding to Pannenburg's glowing description of a new trap for songbirds with: "Perhaps we should examine to what extent this wonderful device elucidates the neurotic projections of its inventors," before breaking into laughter while she quashed a cigarette butt.

Ashtrays filled and beer bottles emptied, and Tanaki experienced the unsettling feeling that he was assuming the role of audience, and that she was performing a high-wire routine for his personal benefit, though he couldn't begin to guess why. He only knew that looking back the next day, all he could remember was watching her through a haze of smoke as she laughed at one of Pannenburg's witticisms, or affected a pensive air, as if she were taking Euler's remarks seriously…

The coffee shop was situated between a laundromat and an insurance agency. Tanaki entered and took a seat at the counter. He ordered a cup of coffee and a sandwich and looked through a newspaper left by an earlier customer. On A-4 he came across the following item:

## WOMAN MAULED BY LIONS

An unidentified woman was found dead early yesterday in the lion pavilion at National Zoo. Her severely mauled body was encountered by two zoo employees who feed the powerful beasts every morning.

The victim's motivation for entering the pavilion isn't clear, and police haven't ruled out the possibility that she was forced into the enclosure against her will. The coroner's office placed the time of death shortly after midnight.

According to Joseph Scalotti, who manages the pavilion, it's likely the large carnivores attacked the woman out of fear or in defense of their territory, since the cats are well fed on a diet of ground horse meat. Nonetheless, it appears that portions of the victim's left arm are missing.

The lion pavilion, constructed in 1979, is not enclosed by bars. A moat twenty feet wide and fifteen feet deep prevents the dangerous predators from escaping. The structure cannot, zoo officials concede, prevent a determined visitor from entering the animals' habitat.

Officials are attempting to determine the woman's identity. According to police, a key found on the body has been traced to an apartment building in Nashville.

Tanaki's sandwich came, he dug in without ceremony. While he finished his coffee, he congratulated himself on having found a place to stay so quickly, the first he'd looked at. The apartment was perfectly suitable, and he resisted the temptation to question whether he'd acted rashly. "Sometimes," he said to himself, "you just get lucky."

He decided to go directly to the research station and get settled in. The season was advancing, and much of his work could be done only during specific phases of the annual cycle. Heron were congregating in their rookeries. Osprey were arriving from points south and would soon begin their elaborate breeding rituals. And if luck were with him it wouldn't be too late to catch the herring runs. And so it went with myriad other animals as well as plants, like the aquatic vegetation that was beginning to grow again in the shoals and marshes. Every new season, every new week, in fact, brought significant changes to an ecosystem. The cycle repeated itself year after year, a cosmic carrousel ride, and an enthralled Tanaki was glad he had a token.

He stood at the rail of the ferry as it puttered its way across the sleepy little river, taking in the breeze coming off the water. A distaff group of mallards were floating near the dock at Benton.

The research station was situated on a narrow point of land that extended like a pseudopod into the bay south of town. Tanaki cruised down the main drag, past the guest inns, restaurants, and gift shops, then pulled into the station's parking lot to the sound of gravel crunching under the Honda's tires.

"You must be Dr. Tanaki," the receptionist said when he entered the lobby.

"It's so hard to be anonymous," he thought, figuring his Asian features had given him away. "David," he said, holding out his hand.

"David then," she said with a friendly smile, placing a sinuous hand in his. "I'm Cynthia. We've been looking forward to your arrival."

He followed her down a dark corridor to a large and open room: surrounded by windows, it offered spectacular views of the bay on three sides. Around its perimeter were laboratories demarcated by partial walls, each occupied by one of the Center's scientists.

The two made the rounds, Tanaki trying to fix names in his memory. Only one of his new colleagues made an impression on him—a marine biologist by the name of Mark DeForrest, a stocky man of medium height with a dark beard, glasses, and a knowing gleam in his eye.

Cynthia showed him other laboratories located throughout the building, some with specialized equipment not available in the scientists' individual labs, also holding pens with sluices emptying into the bay, and a scale model of the estuary. Then she escorted him to Folker's office, located in a wing of its own. Tanaki thanked him for his hospitality and let him know he'd be moving out within the week.

He settled into his lab and began taking an inventory of scientific equipment and supplies, and spent much of the afternoon going back and forth to Cynthia for things he needed.

At one juncture DeForrest's face appeared over the partition of his cubicle.

"Don't be afraid to ask for it—believe me, this place is loaded," he said with that glimmer in his eyes, then disappeared.

Tanaki stayed until late, determined to get his lab in order as soon as possible. He had a feeling the bay was rapidly receding into an inaccessible distance, that there was no time to lose.

# 3

# *Reynolds*

"It *will* be dark around eight."

Reynolds sunk the pole into the thick mud, leaning into it as the boat brushed against the grasses that lined the narrow watercourse. He and Tanaki had floated away from the research station just after first light and it was now approaching four in the afternoon. Tanaki had eagerly wanted to explore the tidal creeks that meander through the marshes south of Benton. It was a pleasant spring day, sunny and clear. When they weren't taking water samples and pulling up bouquets of aquatic plants, he and Reynolds poled and paddled far into a labyrinthine network of interconnecting waterways.

It wasn't long after they'd entered the marshes that Reynolds began to entertain doubts about Tanaki, though he didn't say as much. He'd been working at the station for twelve years and had come to expect a fair degree of level-headedness on the part of the staff. But he couldn't figure this new guy out. Since it was the first time they'd been on the water together, he could understand Tanaki's innocence regarding the difficulty of navigating out of that maze of uncharted creeks. But the scientist's unconcern in the face of Reynolds' efforts to recommend simple precautions left him thoroughly nonplussed. Gleefully examining marsh grasses and lovingly massaging bottom muck in his hands, Tanaki seemed unaware of the passage of time. Hence Reynolds' reminder about the hour of sunset. In fact, it wasn't the first. He'd initially offered this parcel of information around noon, when his thoughts first turned to getting out of the marshes by nightfall.

"It'll be gettin' dark around eight this evening," he'd said, assuming a word to the wise . . .

Then around one.

"Like I said, it gets dark around eight."

At two he'd tried a variation on the theme, as his earlier remarks had failed to elicit the slightest reaction from the biologist.

"We'd better leave enough time to make our way outta here by sunset."

This drew unintelligible mumblings from Tanaki, who was intent upon a vial filled with cloudy marsh water.

Reynolds had lived around the bay for the better part of his sixty-odd years. Descended from a long line of slaves, sharecroppers, and watermen, with an admixture of planter and a slice of Nanticoke Indian to boot, he'd worked on farms as a boy, and took to the water after returning from the war. On their way to the marshes, Tanaki had asked how he came to work at the research station.

"Kept gettin' harder to make a decent living on the water," Reynolds explained. "No more clams, no more oysters . . . all those long faces at the dock at the end of the day. Here there's a regular paycheck."

He was well liked at the Center, with an avuncular manner that especially appealed to the younger staff. He almost seemed part of the bay, with its quiet marshes, perennial fish runs, and regular tides—steady and efficient in his work, neither hurrying nor slacking. He had a lot of patience, but like an old song said, that's a lot to lose. He could deal with spending the night shivering in the marshes if it came to that. But Shirley'd be worried as hell, and how would he face his waterman friends if the Coast Guard had to come after him? Though he hated to dampen the newcomer's enthusiasm—having romanced the estuary for a lifetime, he could imagine Tanaki's excitement on his first date—he figured it was time to speak plainly.

"Listen chief," he said, "if we don't start heading back we'll never get outta here by dark."

"Dark?" Tanaki responded vaguely, hardly shifting his attention from the clump of marsh grass he was examining.

"Normally there wouldn't be any difficulty, but the way you wanted to get in here, I'm not sure about the way out. We'll need to do it by trial and error."

"Trial and error . . ." Tanaki mouthed dreamily.

Reynolds settled into the back of the boat with a deep exhalation. He observed Tanaki, looking for some clue about this guy he'd have to be dealing with. Early to mid-thirties, he figured. Clear skin. Neither thin nor fat. Japanese features. A shock of dark hair falling over a broad forehead. Blue nylon windbreaker and white golf shirt. He marvelled at his concentration: he'd worked with scores of scientists over the years, but had never seen anyone so enraptured with the objects of his study. He was irritated at the difficulty of communicating with the guy, but experienced a sympathetic satisfaction that the young man had found something he could devote himself to with such a whole heart. He focused on the dripping vegetation Tanaki held in his hands and was overwhelmed by a sudden, deep, and inexplicable sense of connection to the new researcher. Then something peculiar happened. The bright glare of the sunlight coming off the marsh penetrated deep into his mind. His vision went hazy and he began hearing phantom sounds, the unmistakable riveting of a machine gun, then terrific explosions.

The next thing he knew Tanaki was shaking him by the shoulders. "Excuse me, Mr. Reynolds. Are you okay?"

Reynolds began to come out of it. He looked dazedly at Tanaki.

"Are you alright?" Tanaki asked again. "Do you have any medical conditions I ought to know about?"

Reynolds shook his head vigorously, forcefully pulling himself back to consciousness. "No, I'm okay," he said, rubbing a large hand across his face.

"Sure you're alright?"

"Don't sweat it," he responded, pulling himself off the boat's bottom, reaching for the seat.

Tanaki fretted as he helped him onto the bench. "Maybe it's just too much sun," he said. Then, brushing dirt off his jacket, "You better see a doctor, get that checked out."

"Sure," Reynolds responded abstractedly.

"We'd better be getting back."

"That's what I've been saying," Reynolds said, rousing himself and looking at his watch. "But it'll be a close thing if we get outta here by dark."

Tanaki squinted over the expanse of the marshes.

"It's around this mound up ahead," he said assuredly, taking up the pole.

"Good guess," Reynolds thought as he responded, "Whatever you say . . ."

But the sun was still riding well over the western shore when they spotted the station's motorboat anchored at the edge of the marshes. Reynolds figured Tanaki had employed some subtle system for marking the route, though he couldn't imagine why the guy would want to mystify the thing—he didn't figure him for the power-trip type. But he was too out-of-sorts to ponder the matter deeply.

The sky was growing dark as the two fastened the motorboat's lines to the station's dock. Tanaki thanked Reynolds and said goodnight.

"Okay Dave . . ." Reynolds responded.

# 4

# *Valerie*

He did a heroic job of putting up a good front, but Tanaki frequently experienced the sensation that he didn't know exactly what he was doing. As if, underlying his day-to-day comings and goings, there was some inner migration taking place. To where, or even from where, he would have been hard-pressed to define, as he would have been hard-pressed to determine whether this migration was, like that of a cabbage moth, one uninterrupted journey from birth to death in a straight line, never returning to the point of departure, or whether it constituted a series of "return" migrations, an endless loop like that of songbirds and waterfowl. He was heading west again, back over the magisterial span of the Bay Bridge, back toward the realm of solid ground, the land of commerce, law and industry. More specifically, he was on his way to Baltimore, where he'd agreed to represent the Center at a conference on environmental problems facing the bay. To his objections that he'd only been on the Shore for three weeks, Folker replied that he knew enough to put on a dog and pony show for the policy wonks who would make up most of the conference's attendance. And of course it was to be expected that the new guy would get stuck with more of the unpleasant chores no one wanted to interrupt their research for. Public relations was part of the job, Folker explained. "Sure, in an ideal world we'd all love to do nothing but pure science, but the unfortunate fact is, we've got to keep some visibility up—that's what keeps the moolah flowing out of Annapolis."

Tanaki was beginning to hate Folker's glib way of dismissing an obvious inconvenience.

"You know how it is," Folker continued. "We've got to get out there and prove we're doing something useful."

Tanaki mulled over Folker's comments as he sped toward Baltimore, dodging the tractor-trailer trucks, trying to maintain a decent speed. One remark in particular struck him in an unexpected way, hinting at a truth about himself he'd been growing into but hadn't taken stock of. When Folker said "we'd all love to do nothing but pure science" he'd sensed a nagging need to qualify the statement, though he didn't voice his feelings, nor would he have known how to limn them at the moment. He'd fallen in love with science once upon a time, and as is usually the case with love affairs, he hadn't stopped to consider where his infatuation was leading him. And though he still mightily loved his research—was sure he always would, in fact—he was beginning to sense that he may have failed to attend to other strata of his being, other aspects of his nature that had continued their own migrations, unheeding of his conscious complicity.

He did regret leaving the Shore, if only for a day. His work was starting nicely: he was getting a feel for the bay: its marshes and tributaries, its fish, water grasses, muskrats, and birds. And he didn't relish being in the city. The intensity of the traffic was already disturbing the calm that came over him his first day on the Shore. It was some consolation at least, as he approached the aquarium on Pratt Street, to see the harbor nudging its way into the metropolis, knowing that this placid space of water was part of the same aquatic web, by way of the Patapsco River, that filled the large windows of his lab with its radiance, its shifting planes of light.

Listening to the moderator introduce him, he looked over the sleekly modern room full of lawyers, nature non-profit staff and journalists. He shuffled through the index cards on which he'd jotted some talking points and realized with a sense of panic that he hadn't figured out how he was going to begin. Out plate glass windows the harbor glistened in the morning sun; his eyes were pulled toward the water. He took in the view. With that image in mind, amid scattered applause, he stepped to the podium. He spoke about the primeval bay's tremendous fecundity, how its vast shoreline and plentiful shoals constitute millions of acres of wetlands, an ecosystem many times more productive than even the most fertile farmland. He grew rhapsodic over the bay's shallow profile, which favors a profusion of bottom vegetation that forms the basis of complex communities of life. He discussed the bay's ever-changing salinity portrait, which allows species that tolerate such variable conditions to thrive and reproduce in fantastic numbers. "As a result of these fortunate circumstances," he said, gesturing toward the harbor, "this estuary has, throughout the millennia, acted as a powerful magnet for migrating fish and waterfowl. As you probably know, it's North America's most productive fishery after the Atlantic and Pacific oceans."

Then he shifted gears. He spoke of the gradual but relentless degradation of the bay environment that had been taking place in modern times. He lamented the scores of species, once extravagantly plentiful, whose numbers were rapidly dwindling. In a voice tinged with sadness he touched on the case of the American shad, whose bountiful spawning runs were once desperately awaited by hungry colonists at the end of lean winters. They were now hardly found in the bay system, their upriver spawning grounds blocked by the giant Conowingo power dam. He spoke of the canvasback duck, once a favorite of Tidewater sportsmen, now seldom encountered around the Chesapeake, due to the decimation of the bottom grasses on which it feeds. He described the problem of over-enrichment from fertilizer run-off and its role in the algae blooms that were smothering life beneath the surface, then gave his audience a primer on sewage disposal and other pressures that a burgeoning human population was placing on the ecosystem. And with a sense of tragedy, he explained the vital role once played by oysters in filtering the estuary's waters, a species whose numbers had fallen to a miniscule fraction of their nineteenth-century levels.

Much of his audience strained to follow his discursive presentation, strewn, as it was, with biological concepts and terminology. But Tanaki held their interest, and surprised himself—he'd never been much of a rhetorician—with the intensifying ardor with which he delivered his remarks. Taking a final look down on the harbor, he closed with reference to a document Folker had provided him, the report of a commission Maryland's governor had convened to evaluate the health of the bay.

"Listen to this," he said, flourishing the report.

"Alarming decline of striped bass stocks. Black duck populations down from three-hundred thousand to thirty-thousand in forty years. Redhead ducks abandoning the bay due to loss of submersed vegetation. PCBs in bluefish, and millions of fish dead from effluent in the James River. Clearing of forests needed by eagles for nesting. Politically directed management of oysters at the behest of harvesters. And get this—repeated warnings of numerous scientists and commissions of inquiry ignored by the Virginia and Maryland legislatures!"

His face was flushed as he stammered out these last remarks, raising the report over his head. Then he fell silent, still holding the report aloft in a Statue of Liberty pose, frozen into a living tableau. The audience sat in mute embarrassment at what seemed an affected attempt at a dramatic close, but it wasn't an act. Tanaki's evocation of the destruction wrought on the bay over the last century had left him in a state of shock, as if he himself had incurred all the violations and assaults he'd described.

Finally a woman stood up in the center of the room. "Dr. Tanaki," she said coaxingly, nudging him from his stupor. "I enjoyed your presentation." Tanaki shook his head and peered out into the room. The woman continued. "Could you tell us, what do you consider the most serious threat to the bay's ecological health?"

He spoke uncertainly as he tried to focus on the indistinct figure, blonde hair delicately braided around the temples, wearing a light green suit. "There are so many . . . Over-enrichment from fertilizer run-off . . . Filling of wetlands . . . Inorganic pollutants . . . Irresponsible harvesting . . . Boats—excuse me if I'm rambling. I'm feeling a little strange."

"You're doing fine," the woman said. The moderator began to rise.

"On a more general level," Tanaki said weakly, but with more focus, "I've heard the situation in the bay characterized as death-by-a-thousand-cuts. An ecosystem is a living entity, it can only take so much abuse. You can kill it with one big blow, or with a series of small but unrelenting ones."

A representative from an industry association rose to speak.

"Mr. Tanaki, can you tell us how long you've been at the Center?"

Sensing a trap, Tanaki hemmed and hawed. Coming to his side, the moderator bailed him out. "I'm afraid that's all the time we have for questions. We've got a very busy agenda. Lunch is to your left as you leave the room."

The woman in green approached Tanaki as people filtered out, holding a cup of water. "Here," she said, "this will help. You alright?" He took a small sip. "I'm better." She introduced herself as Valerie Stanton. On their way to lunch they talked about the bay, and Tanaki began to appreciate a searching mind and a keen awareness of the natural environment. Before splitting up to take their respective seats he'd accepted an invitation to meet for dinner when the conference ended. Following the red sports car with the Chesapeake Bay tag toward Little Italy, he wondered what her take might be. Was she only interested in his ideas on ecology? Or was something else going on? He did find her attractive. She seemed sincere and good-hearted. And she dimly reminded him of someone. Someone from long ago.

He parked behind her on a street lined with trim row houses with formstone facades and marble stoops. A humid breeze engulfed them from the harbor as they walked to a corner restaurant with the modest but pleasant aura of an Italian working-class home of the fifties.

"That was a lame way to end a talk," he said, shaking his head in amused disbelief.

"I wouldn't worry about it. A little drama can leave a lasting impression. Ask any trial lawyer."

Tanaki looked at her doubtfully. "I hope you're right. It's not the kind of thing I normally do—I was more or less corralled into this one."

"But you're good at it," she said, while a waiter poured wine between them. "You should do more advocacy."

"I don't know. Maybe I ought to leave that to you lawyers—or was it law professor?"

"Both, really. I teach environmental law and do some pro bono work on the side."

"Pro bono? You mean like helping some character who doesn't have any money get out of jail?"

"Criminal law isn't my area," she said, "but I'll take on a case when the legal defense project is overloaded. Most of my outside work is environment-related. I've been serving on a commission looking at land use on the coast. I'm also working on a project with the Chesapeake Bay Fund—drafting regulations for fertilizer run-off."

He was beguiled by her interest in fertilizer run-off, but didn't tell her. Instead he said, "Sounds like you're pretty involved."

"It's a big part of my life. Maybe too big, I don't know."

"But you must enjoy legal work."

"It's really more about protecting something I care about."

Tanaki looked down thoughtfully, and as he remained wordless, Valerie continued.

"I grew up in a place called Timonium, which used to be on the outer fringe of the suburbs—now it's engulfed in sprawl. It was rustic out there then, blending into farms and forests. I have such great memories, running barefoot through the neighborhood, or making excursions into the woods with my brothers. My favorite times were summer evenings, playing on the lawns with all the fireflies flashing. The air was clear and fresh. At night there were so many stars . . ."

"Sounds like a happy childhood," he noted wistfully.

"Maybe when I was younger. When I got into my teens everything wasn't so rosy. Vietnam and Nixon, the whole generation gap thing. It seemed a lot of our teachers had given up on us. And at home my parents were having problems—I was a little rudderless for awhile."

"They were strange times for a lot of people."

"Thank God for my friends," she said with more animation. "We'd skip school and go to this abandoned quarry. When it was warm we'd go skinny dipping in one of the pools that had formed. We'd build bonfires and stay into the night, drink cheap wine and smoke stuff I'd be disbarred for today. I realize it was an escape, and some of it was a little reckless, but still there was something terribly beautiful about it."

She must have sensed Tanaki imagining her more reckless behaviors, because she moved abruptly past her adolescent years. "When I was in law school in Charlottesville I did a lot of hiking in the Shenendoahs. Have you ever been down there?"

"No, but I'd love to explore the Appalachian flora system sometime."

"There are such beautiful waterfalls. And the sunsets are amazing. All these hazy blue ranges overlapping one another like palimpsests. We'd always end our hikes at this place call Spittler's Knoll, where the view was unbelievable."

"We?"

"Oh, Ron, this guy I was involved with." Tanaki's silence seemed to beg an explanation. "We were together a few years. You know, I went through a lot of changes for that guy, but he just wasn't ready to make a reasonable commitment." Her eyes were growing moist. "Excuse me," she said, reaching into her purse for tissues. "Allergies."

"They're really awful this time of year," Tanaki said casually. "The trees are still pollinating, and the grasses are starting to come on line. I believe the hickory and sweet vernals are especially active this week."

She nodded appreciatively as she sniffed and daubed at her eyes.

Their dinners came and they chatted about the conference, their opinions of the other presenters, and about the bay. Over spumoni ice cream she attempted to extract a *curriculum vitae* from her companion, but he was feeling reticent, still shaken by his experience at the conference.

"Science, that's me in a nutshell," he said, vaguely aware of the unflattering metaphor. "I live for my work. That's the way it's been since grad school."

"I'll bet there's more to it than that."

Tanaki blushed as he polished off his wine. "I don't know."

They stood on the curb to say goodnight. Valerie gave him a warm hug and said she'd like to get together again, both of which pleased him. Driving home he kept seeing her pale blue eyes.

When he got back to his apartment he switched on the black and white TV that sat on a shaky table, the only piece of furniture in the living room besides a stuffed chair he'd bought at a secondhand shop in town. His attention was immediately riveted by horrific images of a bloodied and prostrate black swan while a female anchor voiced-over the story.

"The National Zoo is in the news again today as yet another encounter between man and animal leaves zoo officials, police and concerned citizens reeling. An Australian black swan, one of the zoo's prized possessions, was found dead this morning in the waterfowl pavilion. It appears that the nineteen-pound bird, which had lived at the zoo for six years, was deliberately killed by a blow to the head with a large stone found nearby. Police are holding a fifteen-year-old male in the incident. He turned himself in this evening at the third precinct headquarters, feeling remorse over his part in the slaying, in which he claims to have participated with two other youths. According to sources, the teenager gave no reason for killing the bird other than "he just felt like it." Since they're juveniles, the names of all three suspects are being withheld. It remains unclear whether the incident is related to the fatal mauling of a Tennessee woman by the zoo's lions last month."

"Damn!" Tanaki whispered, stunned. He'd always considered the Australian black to be one of the most gorgeous creatures on the planet. Observing them at close range in Tasmania, he'd never tired of their elegant beauty. He desperately wanted more information, but when the broadcast resumed after a commercial the announcer moved to a story about a neighborhood clinic closing.

He went to bed in a dark mood and was soon engulfed in dream. He stood at the edge of a beautiful pool surrounded by rushes and flowers, watching a black swan glide over the surface. The man-made pond, designed with a perfect balance of nature and artifice, pleased him immensely. He turned at the sound of a loud noise, but seeing nothing, turned again to the pool. The swan had disappeared. Instead Valerie cut through the water in a skimpy black bikini, beckoning him to jump in. He walked onto a delicately arching footbridge and encountered Mrs. Scofield, fearfully pleading with him to go no further. He looked over the pond, seeking Valerie, but saw only a bloody streak running through the water. The scene shifted. He was standing beside the highway, a crisp breeze blowing through his hair. There was a car on the shoulder with its trunk open. Mrs. Scofield sat inside, licking her lips in an incredibly suggestive way. He took a step, another, then found himself enfolded in Valerie's waiting arms. He was awakened by a coolness running down his thigh. "Oh God," he said in a tone suggesting both pleasure and inconvenience, then limped stiffly to the bathroom.

# 5

# *Folker*

By the time the azaleas on Talbot Street had arrayed themselves in scarlet, with the green of the marshes burgeoning forth with an amazing profligacy, Tanaki was finding his stride. He'd made several trips into the bay with Reynolds; exploring swamps, oyster reefs, shoals, and creeks; taking water and plant samples; sighting birds, catching fish, checking crab pots, and peeking into ospreys' nests. Eager to jump-start his research, he spent most evenings at the lab evaluating samples and writing up results. He was coming to grips with the task of reducing the web of migration in and out of, and within, the bay to some kind of intelligible schema.

He started where he had to start, getting a feel for the various habitats and observing the animals when possible. As the season advanced he'd concentrate more on particular species as they underwent critical phases of their life cycles. Summer-resident birds would be nesting and breeding, raising the year's young, undergoing a moult, then experiencing a slew of other bodily changes in preparation for the migratory journeys of the fall. A number of fish species were entering the estuary, some to spawn in the relative safety of the bay and its tributaries, others to take advantage of the eruption of plant and animal life, much of it on the planktonic level, that characterized the estuary's warmer months. Meanwhile a host of migratory dramas would occur entirely within the bay, like that of the blue crab, whose mated females, having been romanced for the first and only time in their lives, would be clawing their way along the shoals towards the Virginia Capes to spawn, as young of the prior year passed them on their journeys up-bay where they would grow to maturity.

Not long after the Baltimore conference Tanaki experienced what was to be the first of many puzzling encounters with Folker. It was established protocol for the Center's researchers to keep Folker informed where they worked on a day-to-day basis, in case for some reason one of them were not to return to the Center. The bay's waters, after all, weren't always benign, and Tanaki's enthusiasm would have gotten him into trouble on a couple of occasions had it not been for Reynolds' seasoned prudence.

But Tanaki was unaware of any storm warnings on a bright Friday morning when he stopped by Folker's office to let him know that he and Reynolds were heading toward Smith Island, where he planned to take a look at the salt grass meadows that extend underwater for thousands of acres like aquatic prairies in the lower reaches of the estuary.

Folker's face clouded with consternation. "Listen, Dave. I'm real sorry, but that portion of the bay's off-limits now. Why don't you head north? There're some nice underwater beds up around Elk Neck."

"But Guy," Tanaki responded quizzically, "you know that's a completely different habitat from down in the lower bay. The salinity portraits aren't even close."

"Sorry, Dave. Them's the rules. What can I say?"

"Is the weather predicted to turn bad?" Tanaki hardly managed to mask his irritation.

"Could be, you never know. Anyhow, I've really got to get back to work." Folker displayed the scattered papers on his desk with an outstretched hand.

"Fine," Tanaki replied, gritting his teeth as he turned to go.

"Oh, and Dave," Folker called from within the office.

Tanaki wheeled a couple of steps and leaned into the doorway, grasping the doorjamb with one hand. "Yes?"

"I've got another dog and pony show I need someone for. Some nice little old ladies who happen to be some of our most active supporters."

"But . . ." Tanaki began to protest, thinking of the intensifying schedule of research on his plate. While he hesitated Folker added, "Sorry, old man, you were such a hit at the last meeting. I didn't know we were hiring such a good front man."

Tanaki didn't respond. But as he walked through the narrow hallway toward his lab he grumbled to himself, an occasional word emerging into audibility, had there been anyone to hear it.

" . . . arbitrary! . . ."

" . . . stupid! . . ."

" . . . bullshit!"

He had to content himself with this private venting of frustration; it would have been unlike him to blow up at work. It's true that his parents—especially his father—had been given every encouragement, while growing up, to master an American cultural idiom that had eluded his grandparents. But some traditions die harder then others, and his father had never ceased to remind him of the old Japanese proverb: *The nail that sticks up gets hammered down.* In fact, the phrase now came floating into his mind involuntarily, like some importunate harpy.

"I'd like to hammer something alright," he thought to himself as he entered the open area surrounded by his colleagues' labs. Crossing the sunlit room toward his cubicle he ran into DeForrest, whom he'd failed to notice in his self-absorption.

"Whoa, Nelly," DeForrest joked. "Where's the fire?"

DeForrest's mirth was like a splash of cold water on Tanaki, calling him back from his preoccupations.

"Sorry, Mark. Folker has just messed up my entire work schedule."

"Well," DeForrest said, "join the club."

"It's happened to you?"

"It's happened to all of us. You see," he resumed, speaking more quietly, "the problem is the guy's clueless, doesn't know a thing about what we're doing here. He sits in his gold-plated office surrounded by his precious paperwork, making pronouncements about how we've got to keep the bucks coming out of Annapolis and prove we're useful and all that bunk. Annapolis, sure he's interested in Annapolis. He's some kind of political appointment, after all. Tell me," he continued, "had you ever heard of the guy before you came here?"

"Well, in fact, I was a little concerned about that."

"Neither has anyone else. That should tell you something right there. No reputation in the field whatsoever. Why he's here nobody knows. And all this obstructionism, it's unprecedented in my experience; and I've been around a few years, if you know what I mean. Anyhow, none of us really get it, but I'm starting to think there's something fishy about the whole thing—no pun intended."

"Listen," he continued. "What story did he give you? Weather? Turbulence? Too many ocean freighters out there?"

"He didn't give any explanation at all."

"Now that's unusual," DeForrest replied, stroking his beard. "Maybe he's completely lost it."

# 6

# The Yamaguchis

As Tanaki prepared for a long evening at the lab he felt a sense of depletion. His dust-up with Folker had dented his morale, precipitating a bottoming out already brewing on account of his herculean work schedule. After staring mindlessly at the bay for half an hour from the chair in his cubicle he decided to head home. He'd hardly been in his apartment since the move, and figured a quiet evening would do him some good.

There was a warm southerly breeze coming off the water when he left the station. He stopped by the market to pick up some spaghetti and bottled sauce. He sat on an orange crate in the dining nook, looking at the magnolias while forking the slippery noodles off of one of the two dinner plates he owned.

It was quiet on the street except for the songs of birds. It felt good to look around and realize that he'd made two good decisions—to take the apartment, and to furnish it sparingly. It was like a vacuum, a vacuum that sucked up all the striving that marked his existence lately.

He put the plate in the sink and made himself comfortable in his easy chair, turning over the cover of a scientific journal that had lain unopened by the door since it arrived a week earlier. He smiled when he noticed an article by Moeller in the contents. It somehow confirmed the validity of his decision to knock off early. Its title: "Competing philosophical angles on the current migrational evolutionary paradigm."

"Sounds like he's at it again," he thought: Moeller had a reputation for taking hard science beyond its normal boundaries; he'd witnessed plenty of his famously speculative flights over beers and coffee in cafes along the North Sea coast. In the middle of the following passage (which he couldn't help but hear in Moeller's refined German accent): "Is it really true that in the evolutionary game there are only winners and losers; with no exiguous pay-offs? . . ." he was interrupted by a knock at the door.

Expecting his landlady, he blenched at finding two younger women—Japanese in appearance—standing on the landing. The one who introduced herself as Setsuko Yamaguchi was elegant and thin, radiating confidence. She introduced her companion, shy and softly rounded, as her sister Nariko.

"We just came by to say hello," Setsuko said in accented but assured English.

He smiled weakly, holding the journal at his side.

"We live up on the third floor. Mrs. Stafford said you were new in town. We'd love to have you to dinner sometime."

"That's nice of you," he said formally, thinking of his pressing work schedule.

"How about tomorrow evening? It is Saturday. You know, all work no play makes Jack a dull boy."

"That might be possible," he offered hesitantly.

"Great! See you at six. Ciao!"

He groped for a rejoinder while she wheeled gaily toward the staircase. Nariko, embarrassed by her sister's audaciousness, bowed awkwardly and turned to follow. Tanaki returned the gesture and closed the door. He stood dumbfounded, wondering what had happened. "Odd," he thought, "just when I'm trying to have a quiet evening."

He made his way back to the easy chair but couldn't focus on Moeller's article. Something about those two women was tugging at him. Something to do with their Japanese-ness. It was an odd coincidence for one thing, and odd coincidences always made him nervous. There was also the possibility they'd look to him as a protecting sponsor, just because they shared a common ethnic ancestry. That made him even more nervous. He had a hard time believing it was simply a matter of good fortune that two attractive and friendly women happened to be living upstairs. He cogitated the matter until he got tired of going in circles around it, then settled back into his chair and lost himself in the journal.

When he awoke in the morning, after a night of heavy and luxuriant sleep, he found himself looking forward to the get-together. He couldn't deny there'd been something missing in his life, something having to do with being with people—not to work with them, but to feel their presence, hear their voices, smell their scents. He spent most of the day at the lab, ran a few errands, then made his way past the cigar store Indian and up the creaking stairs to the third floor, carrying a bottle of wine he'd picked up at the corner market.

Setsuko answered the door with a welcoming smile and thanked him for the wine with a quick bow. "Please come in," she said with a refined inflection. "Nari's in the kitchen. Make yourself comfortable while we finish dinner."

He removed his shoes and placed them on a shelf by the door beside several small pairs he surmised belonged to the Yamaguchis. He looked around the living room. It was furnished in a spare Japanese style, with paper fans and classic prints on the walls. It was unclear how the effect had been achieved, but there was a warm, reddish glow, as if the room had absorbed the colors of a thousand sunsets. Perhaps it had something to do with the highly polished floor, the wood of which was of a reddish hue. Then again, the orange light of the dying day may have been responsible.

Tatami mats surrounded a low table in the center of the room.

Tanaki sat down on one and stared intently at a print depicting a white crane flying over a snow covered forest. He was immersed in thoughts of the bird's life-cycle when Setsuko and Nariko emerged from the kitchen through a cloud of steam.

"Excuse us while we do a brief service before dinner," Setsuko said.

He had no idea what she was referring to but didn't ask.

The women moved to a table before a window facing the Choptank, through which Tanaki saw fragments of nacred water through the trees in the neighboring yards. The room was growing dark. Nariko lit some candles. She and Setsuko knelt before the table, apparently an altar of some kind. It supported a magnificent color photo of a blue marlin, and a delicately carved frame bearing the portrait of an elderly man with an open face and kind eyes. A sprig of loblolly pine lay across the front of the table. There were also flowers and a sake cup which Nariko filled with a decanter she'd carried from the kitchen. The women knelt silently for a few minutes before beginning to intone a sing-songy chant in soft, high-pitched voices. Tanaki remained seated on his mat, looking at the photos on the altar, then out the window toward the river, then at Setsuko and Nariko. He couldn't understand a word of the chants, never having learned Japanese. But the strange sounds affected him nonetheless, along with the reddish glow in the room, the candlelight, the pungent aroma of seared seafood coming from the kitchen, and the shards of river out the window. He began to feel, though he would have hesitated to use the word, spiritual. When he tried to objectify the experience he could only identify a kind of pulsing, a pulsing that linked him with the sisters, the sunset, the river, the marlin in the photograph, and the old man with the kind eyes whom he was sure he'd never seen before.

When after five minutes the sisters fell into silent meditation he noticed something unusual. It was as though the sound of their voices were still in the room. Perhaps not the sound per se, not even a reverberation or an echo. But he sensed some quality that hadn't been there when he came in, a substance that occupied every molecule of air. And he connected it with the red-dish glow he'd noted earlier. It made him feel a little off-center, but curious to explore the phenomenon further. When Setsuko sprang to her feet and began rearranging the ritual paraphernalia he felt almost cheated.

"Ready to eat?" she asked matter-of-factly as she and Nariko headed toward the kitchen. Before he could respond they returned with two large platters loaded with seafood delicacies that he soon learned were cooked to perfection.

"Where'd you get this seafood?" he asked by way of compliment.

"We've got a very special source," Setsuko hinted solemnly. Nariko reddened and pressed her lips tightly, as if suppressing an urge to laugh.

"Is it a secret?" he asked, going along with the game.

"Oh no, it's no secret," Setsuko said, gazing soulfully toward the river, her chopsticks suspended before her. Tanaki looked baffled and quit chewing a mouthful of squid.

"We got it . . . from the sea!" Setsuko finally blurted out in an eruption of laughter she shared with Nariko, leaving Tanaki blushing at the thought of having been so amusing to his hostesses.

As the laughter subsided, Nariko began shyly. "We . . . joke . . . too much."

Tanaki now realized why Setsuko did the talking. Nariko's English was halting and unsteady. She continued uncertainly. "We have . . . a . . . seafood business."

"Seafood business," Tanaki repeated, pincering a piece in his chopsticks. "Looks like a variety of sea bream," he added, exam-ining the dangling morsel.

"You certainly know your fish," Setsuko replied.

"I am a biologist," he said.

"A biologist," Setsuko purred as she and Nariko exchanged a meaningful look, continuing the cryptic tone they seemed to find amusing.

"This isn't found in the Chesapeake, is it?" Tanaki asked, scrutinizing another piece, anxious to break up a species of conspiracy he didn't understand.

"Oh no," Setsuko said, "we take it off-shore."

"Special . . . delicacy," Nariko added, as she chewed a mouthful of the delectable animal.

"It's considered good luck, especially for fishermen," Setsuko explained.

"People say it's . . ." Nariko struggled.

"Auspicious," Setsuko offered. "That print by the kitchen," she said, mixing sauces in a small bowl, "it's the god *Ebisu*, patron of fishermen. You can see the sea bream under his left arm."

Tanaki looked past Nariko's head to the portrait of the god. It depicted a stoutly built figure with flaring eyes and a top knot, a flowing kimono swirling around him. He was surrounded by the kind of stylized waves Tanaki remembered seeing in a print that everyone had on their wall at college. Beyond him a red *torii* rose from the sea. In the distance, snow-capped mountains. The god strode through the waves wearing an expression of wild glee, his step an exuberant dance.

"So all this came from your seafood business?" Tanaki asked, turning his attention again to his dinner.

"Well," Setsuko began, "actually father's business."

"Good old *chi-chi*," Nariko added, her tone tinged with homesickness.

"But we're in charge of Chesapeake operations," Setsuko continued. "We have twenty ships. We started with two."

"My sister is . . . good . . . businesswoman," Nariko added.

"It sounds that way," Tanaki replied, sipping sake.

"Seafood is big business in Japan, of course," Setsuko said. "But this was my idea, the Chesapeake operation. It's funny. Though I'd never been here before, from the earliest age I felt a bizarre attraction to the bay. Especially colonial times, the English settlers and all that. I read about it in the encyclopedia and did school projects on the subject. Then after university, when I got involved with father's business, I begged and pleaded—observing the best filial devotion, of course—until he agreed to set up an operation here. Naturally I ran the numbers and convinced him it made business sense to cut out the middleman."

After collecting the dinner plates the women excused themselves and disappeared into the kitchen. They returned with a Japanese tea service. While they were setting out the cups, Tanaki heard their chanting voices echoing back from some unknown region of his consciousness. The sensation was so real, and increased in force to a point where he was compelled to ignore the discretion he'd always been taught was appropriate where other folks' religions were involved.

"What religion is that—with the chanting—if you don't mind my asking?"

Setsuko took a long, luxurious sip and said matter-of-factly, "It's one of the new religions."

"New religions?"

"It was part of the rush hour of the gods."

"I don't think I've heard—I was brought up Episcopalian."

"Are you saying you don't know much about Japan?"

He wasn't sure what he felt as he replied, "My family's pretty American."

"I see," she said, as if she didn't quite believe him. She daubed sauces onto a piece of fish as she explained. "After the war, in Japan, there was a lot of confusion and soul-searching. A bunch of new religions got started. There were so many in the fifties one guy called it rush hour of the gods."

Nariko nodded in agreement. "It's about *kami*," she said.

"*Kami?*"

"*Kami* means something like spirit," Setsuko said. "It's a Shinto term."

"Shinto," Tanaki asked, "isn't that nature worship?"

"*Kami* is in mountains, trees, rivers," Nariko said.

"But also in ancestors and buddhas," Setsuko added.

"So this is a form of Buddhism?" Tanaki asked, seeking solid ground.

"Not really," Setsuko asserted. "Buddhist doctrines do play a role, though."

"It's called—" Nariko began, turning to Setsuko and speaking a Japanese phrase.

"Something like pure action," Setsuko said. "A guy named Ato Matsunawa started it in the forties."

"Wait. He started a religion?"

"Here's the story," Setsuko said. "Ato-san grew up in a fishing village in the north. When he was a teenager his father was killed in the war, leaving the family in his hands. After praying to the *kami* for relief, Ato-san went to work for one of the big fishing companies. He kept praying to the *kami*, and invented the modern method for netting shrimp. He made a killing in the process—in more ways than one, you could say."

Tanaki tipped his cup in acknowledgement of the quip.

"He started a religion based on respect for the *kami*, and before long he had thousands of converts, including our father. Dad had just started his own business. He hadn't even met Mom. After joining Ato-san's sect his profits went through the roof! Now he's always saying how we owe everything to the *kami*, how we have to appreciate what they've done for us."

"Could the bay be considered a *kami*?" Tanaki asked.

"The bay is a huge *kami*," Nariko asserted unhesitatingly.

"Some people call it the shrimp religion," Setsuko said.

"At least it's not . . . the . . . golf religion," Nariko added.

"Golf religion?" Tanaki asked over the sisters' laughter. He was feeling mystified. And certain he was being sucked into something. Something not necessarily unpleasant. Just something.

# 7

# *Birdwatchers*

The hotel was a Georgian structure of whitewashed board surrounded by spreading elms. Tanaki was here to dispatch Folker's latest interruption of his research, a talk before the Chesapeake Avian Support League—the "nice little old ladies" the director had referred to.

Helen Conway was waiting in the lobby when he arrived. Short and of medium build, with soft gray hair drawn partly behind her head, she moved with a fluidity that belied Folker's description. And though she impressed Tanaki as being smartly dressed, there was about her clothing a Bohemian sentimentality, an almost gypsy wildness, that betrayed her identification with the flighted world. Silken scarf. Floral blouse under a loose-fitting tailored jacket. Translucent eyeglasses rising to points at the sides. Her speech was softly articulate.

"Most of our members are long-time residents of the Shore," she explained as they rounded a corner towards the meeting room, "though we're getting a lot of retirees these days. Escaping those dreadful cities across the bay, I suppose."

Tanaki grunted earnestly.

"Our members are quite active in the conservation scene," she continued. "Most belong to several organizations—you know, Audubon, Sierra, Greenpeace."

Tanaki nodded politely, careful not to betray his bemusement at the thought of some quaint ladies in a provincial back-water spearheading the fight against despoilers of the earth. He couldn't imagine that Helen, judging from her demeanor, was brewing up a cauldron of activism on the Shore. More likely, he figured, he'd be addressing what could only be described as a bird-watching club, a coterie of gals who occasionally tiptoed to the edge of a marsh to thrill at the sight of a red-winged blackbird, a diversion from the normal round of coffee klatches and church bazaars.

Not that he felt any aversion to people who simply liked birds. And the subject matter was a cakewalk: judging from Folker's brief remarks, they were expecting some kind of talk on migration. He figured the club was appreciative to have an expert—a real scientist—spend some time with them. He was starting to feel like a damned nice guy.

When he and Helen arrived at the Wicomico Room, a crowd of ladies were in their seats, chatting together or politely waiting. As he looked them over, observing the collection of shiny or dumpy handbags, the funny hats, a couple with small bits of netting, he felt a certain pity, a pity tinged with tenderness. And he noted the ways in which each of them, like Helen, had been transformed through her fascination with birds. There was a plump little wren, a lanky, almost aristocratic egret, a boisterous mockingbird, a sleek swallow, a silent owl.

Helen introduced him to the group; he stepped to the front and casually leaned an elbow on the podium. Having scraped through the Baltimore assignment, he hadn't reflected on what he might say to the ladies until he was on his way to the hotel, not wanting to spend precious research time putting together a talk. Nor had he looked at the information packet Folker had given him. After all, if the closest thing to a religion he possessed was biology, migration was his personal mantra, and he figured he could easily throw out enough interesting tidbits to charm the roll-up stockings off his quaint auditors.

"You know," he began, "we once used the term *migration* only to refer to those spectacular, thousand-mile journeys, like you've seen on National Geographic TV specials."

"Never watch TV," the wren piped up. "It's a complete waste of time."

"Half of it's sordid," added the egret.

"The other's infantile," said the bunting.

Helen Conway sat near the front, smiling benignly.

Tanaki chuckled pleasantly, trying not to lose momentum.

"Good point," he said. "But as I was saying, now we migration guys look at all sorts of movement, actually any movement, no matter how small, by any form of life, as migration."

The ladies stared blankly. He forced an edge of excitement into his voice.

"An amoeba," he said, pinching together his thumb and index finger, "imagine this microscopic organism, painstakingly displacing its miniscule body by the extension of its pseudopods, looking for a more promising solute . . . or even a spore from a tree, floating on the wind, waiting to drop onto a fresh patch of soil, it's all considered part of migration now!"

"We knew that," said the mockingbird, her voice slicing through the room like a stainless steel scalpel.

"You've been doing some reading," Tanaki replied (while thinking to himself, *there's always one wiseacre in the crowd*).

He decided to up the ante. "But have you considered the idea that we humans migrate? And I'm not referring to major episodes of transhumance" (he figured this last term would throw the know-it-alls off the scent) "but I mean any human movement, including your simple trip to the corner grocery."

"Of course," the grackle rasped from a back corner of the room.

A little flustered now, Tanaki gave up all pretense to linearity and began riffing in the general key of animal migration. Somewhere in the melange of words there was something about whales moving between Antarctic feeding grounds and warm water birthing territories; about the flight of the diminutive black poll warbler over a thousand miles of open ocean; about the movement of beehives, the swarming of locusts, and the free flights of such "aerial plankton" as aphids.

It was the owl who finally interrupted him, stating calmly but firmly, "Now *you're* starting to sound like a National Geographic special," instigating a round of laughter that broke the tension of Tanaki's disjointed monologue.

Inspired by her cohort, the swallow said, "But what does all this have to do with conservation? We're a *conservation* group."

"Conservation?"

"Yes," said the bunting, "we were hoping you'd say something about Operation Recovery. Don't you know our group's an authorized participant in the Atlantic flyway banding project?"

"You work with Operation Recovery?" he asked incredulously. The ladies shook their heads in unison. He looked at Helen.

"Perhaps Guy didn't forward our information along."

"I must have missed it," he said, then added, somewhat disoriented, "The data you're helping compile is incredibly important to understanding bird migrations and the effects of habitat loss on bird populations."

He took a couple of steps away from the podium and thought for a moment. Then he resumed conversationally. "I got a call from a friend of mine the other day," he said. "He's been studying obstacles birds face in their migrations. He'd just counted over a thousand starling cadavers around the base of a radio tower in Ohio—if you can believe it, they all collided with it in a single night."

"Oh my"— the swallow.

"Poor things," added the egret.

"But doesn't it just show how high the stakes are?" the black-bird said authoritatively.

"Well—yes," Tanaki replied. "Exactly . . ."

"After all," a warbler chimed in, "migration's no pleasure cruise. These animals need to escape cold, find food, or suitable habitats for rearing their young. It's a matter of life or death—the very viability of the species."

"I couldn't have said it better," Tanaki responded with surprise. "In fact, it's a basic premise of my field that migrants wouldn't undergo all these risks and rigors if an easier avenue to survival existed."

The ladies sat quietly.

"One thing I think migrating animals have going for them," he continued, "is their tendency toward gregariousness. Even species that typically spend their days in solitude will come together when it's time to migrate—due to the hazards of the journey, the exigencies of the mating process—perhaps for reasons we don't fully understand." The ladies' expressions were turning listless. "But you probably know that," he conceded, wishing he'd looked at Folker's packet.

To his relief, Helen stood up, took him by the arm, and warmly thanked him for the lecture. Then she led him into an adjoining room where refreshments were laid out on draped tables. The ladies surrounded him as he sipped a glass of punch, and peppered him with questions on the details of his research, quizzing him on air currents, incubation rates, salinity gradients, freshwater flows, and the growth rates of aquatic vegetation. He was diffident at first, feeling the fool for having misjudged them so completely. But as he fielded their queries, he warmed to the exchange until he was downright happy he'd come. And he began to feel they liked him. They hovered around him as he satisfied their scientific curiosity in extensive detail, and by the time he was preparing to leave, as they nibbled cookies and chatted casually together, he experienced the odd sensation that they were looking at him as if *he* were a bird—some displaced nestling who needed understanding and a little nurturing. He couldn't explain it, but he felt as though he'd been taken into a new flock.

# 8

# Ocean City

Cynthia buzzed Tanaki to let him know Valerie Stanton was on the line.

The call came as a surprise—caught up in a rapidly evolving season of research, Tanaki hadn't had much chance to think about Valerie since the Baltimore meeting. Every now and then, while floating through some marshy creek with Reynolds, a pleasant recollection of their dinner in Little Italy crossed his mind. But if he'd thought about calling her once or twice, the occasion never seemed propitious. He picked up the phone while looking over the bay's waters, blue under the intense June sun.

"Is this David?"

He felt off-base for not having called. Though that wasn't the man's role these days, maybe it had been rude not to venture the gesture. Her voice was free of reproach, but he had a hard time getting started.

"Valerie . . . yeah . . . Hi."

"I'm going out to Ocean City this Saturday," she said. "There are some issues I'm dealing with on the commission, and I wanted to see things with my own eyes."

"I've always said that's the best way to do it."

"I'd rather go to Rehobeth—it's so much quieter. But it's an excuse to get out of town, and it looks like the weather'll be great. I thought you might like to drive out with me. I'll be coming past Cambridge. I can easily stop by for you."

She made it seem casual, not hinting at anything intimate, while not ruling it out. He reflected that he'd been meaning to get to the coast anyway, to the great islands of shifting sand that constitute the shore's vanguard against the relentless pounding of the Atlantic surf. He also remembered her attractive figure and kind eyes, so with a comment about scientific interest that didn't rule out other kinds of interest, he gave her directions and told her he'd be ready Saturday morning.

He recognized the red sports car when it pulled up to the curb, and grabbing his overnight bag, bounded down the steps with only a passing glance at the cigar store Indian. She drove like an ace and didn't bother with the speed limits. Her eyes were hidden behind large shades. Strokes of white along her neck betrayed an earlier application of suntan lotion. The top was down and her golden hair flew in the wind.

They arrived at the coast in little over an hour. It was apparent that Valerie knew Ocean City well. She negotiated the erratic traffic that clotted the main thoroughfare without flinching, then maneuvered onto a side street where she found a coveted parking space near the beach. As for the great barrier island, there wasn't much of it to be seen, most of it having long ago been covered with hotels, restaurants, honky-tonks, boutiques, and a broad swath of asphalt that carried a never-ending flow of cars up and down its length.

Tanaki and Valerie crossed the boardwalk and made their way across the hot sand of the wide beach. Valerie looked around with an arm-spreading gesture that betokened animal health and said, "Don't you love the sun?"

Tanaki meanwhile was adjusting to the brightness, trying to shake himself out of a reverie that had overtaken him on the bridge over the Assowoman Bay, a placid body of water separating the barrier island from the mainland. Looking over its waters he'd drifted into a series of speculations focused on levels of salinity, tides, and water temperature. Now, as he and Valerie walked down the beach toward the surf, the distinctive rhythm of which was already playing on his consciousness, he became aware of the holiday horde that covered the sand with their blankets and umbrellas. He'd spent the previous summer in the far north, observing tundra swans in their breeding grounds, and most of the fall and winter in a small Michigan town waiting to hear about the Chesapeake grant. The presence of so many people startled him.

They spent the day sunbathing, making heroic forays into the freezing surf, and listening to pop tunes on Valerie's boom box. Occasionally she perused a report she'd brought along, something about land use on the coast. Tanaki, for his part, wasn't interested in reading. When they weren't in the water, he lay on his side gazing incredulously at the sea of shining bodies spread under the baking sun, or sat facing the water, watching the swimmers, rafters, and body-surfers.

Valerie closed the report on itself and sat up. "It's amazing to think that a hundred years ago there wasn't anything out here besides a few cottages," she said, looking northward, where towering condos rose one after another.

"No kidding?" Tanaki replied, following her gaze.

"There was no way to get here until they ran a railroad line. Then vacationers from Washington and Baltimore could ferry across the bay and catch the train the rest of the way."

Children careened by the blanket, spraying sand across Tanaki's legs. He brushed it off with emphatic swats. Valerie set the report down, adjusted her hair band, and gazed into the ocean.

"It was still quaint into the forties, though—just a few hotels and fishing camps. Then they put up the Bay Bridge."

"And the swarms came," Tanaki announced like the narrator of a cheap sci-fi flick, looking around at the crowd.

Valerie laughed. "See that barge out there?" she asked, pointing to a fuzzy bar suspended in the haze.

He squinted through the brightness.

"It's part of a Sisyphian effort to prevent erosion of the shoreline."

"I can imagine," he replied. "A barrier island's got to be one of the most fragile landforms on the planet."

"I guess we're into your area of expertise, aren't we?"

"No—please go on, I like to hear you tell it."

"In addition to being so fragile," she said, "this island's in the middle of the Atlantic storm zone."

"Of course!" he replied.

"A big hurricane came through in 1933. Slashed right through. That's where the inlet is now."

"Wait'll a *really* big one comes."

"Exactly what the meteorologists are saying. They say when the big one hits, the whole place may be history."

A gull squawked loudly.

"I suppose the barge is doing some kind of dredging work," Tanaki said.

"Yeah. They pump sand onto the beach from offshore, through these plastic tubes. You should see them. They look like the tentacles of some weird sea monster lying across the beach, one end disappearing into the surf."

"Attack of the sea tubes," he jested in his movie voice, just to hear her laugh again, then resumed more seriously. "Can they really take on Mother Nature with a couple of barges and some plastic tubes?"

"Good question. It seems like every other year there's a story about a big storm erasing an entire season's restoration work."

He nodded knowingly.

"But the town keeps pouring money into erosion control," she concluded. "This place is big business. The economy depends on the beach—obviously."

They fell silent, struck by the extent to which man will go to secure his pleasures, regardless how ephemeral the structures upon which they're built.

Then, as she had throughout the afternoon, she pulled down the straps of her suit and had him cover her back with suntan lotion. When, in spite of these ministrations, her shoulders began turning an unhealthy shade of pink, they gathered up the blanket and headed toward the boardwalk. After browsing in a few shops they returned to the car. They decided to get a room, speaking only of a place to shower and change. They bathed and dressed—she in a slinky number that really showed off her figure—and walked to a breezy dining spot on the sound. Over beers she said a little sheepishly, "Last time we dined I think I told you about my high school wildnesses—I may have even touched on my big heartbreak."

"Oh, I took extensive notes."

She looked at him wryly.

"As a biologist, I'd be remiss if I didn't fully document all new life-forms."

"So the women you date," she said with a fetching smile, "they're just so many interesting specimens?"

He'd taken enough tests to know that the answer to this question was none of the above. "Scratch the bit about the notes," he said. "But I remember the hazy ridges, the fireflies."

She was pleased he'd passed the test, also that he remembered—it showed in her blush. But she didn't want to talk about her life again. Tonight she was determined to find out who was behind the thick glasses, the shock of dark hair falling onto his forehead, a man who, she'd learned on the beach, could watch hovering gulls for twenty minutes as if nothing else existed.

"You must love observing animals."

"I suppose I do."

"Is it all connected with your work?"

"Yes, but it goes back beyond that—probably to the fishing trips I used to take with my father on the Upper Peninsula."

"I hear it's beautiful there."

"Very rugged."

"You'd go fishing with your Dad?"

"When he started taking me I was actually too small to fly fish, five or six. But he'd let me carry his tackle box when we explored up and down streams, looking for a good spot. I'd sit and watch him cast his line." He directed his eyes obliquely across the table, observing something unseen to Valerie. "He knew everything about trout. He'd tell me stuff as he fished. Their habits, what they'd do, where they'd turn up. To me it was like a game. I'd try to figure out what the fish were thinking so we could win." He returned to her eyes. "You know how kids are."

They fell into a moment of quiet beer sipping. Tanaki inhaled and took in his surroundings. The deck on which he sat with Valerie hung over the sound. There was a magenta wash over the water and a cooling breeze. Valerie looked beautifully flushed with the sun and exercise she'd taken during the day; he unthinkingly allowed his gaze to rest languidly across her body. She spoke to break the spell, she wasn't ready for this kind of connection, not until she knew she wasn't another specimen. "I know so little about migration," she said—"just what I've seen on National Geographic specials."

"Funny you mention that."

"Why?"

"Oh, nothing," he said with a small laugh. "But there's a lot more to it than most people think."

"I enjoy complexity."

"I don't suppose you've heard of Aldo Perdecci?"

"Aldo?"—

"Perdecci—it was reading about his work, when I was at Cornell, that got me hooked on migration studies."

"Hooked? That's a pretty strong word."

"I guess it is," he conceded. "It's hard to explain."

"But it started with this—Perdecci?"

"Yes. Before him, everybody thought migration was simple. The classic idea was that animals operate on raw instinct, without any real deliberation involved."

"Kind of like dating."

Tanaki laughed. "That could make for an interesting analysis."

"But not tonight," she said. "I'd rather you tell me about migration."

Tanaki was delighted with her sense of humor, a playful Valerie she seemed to have put on with the slinky dress and earrings. He was also glad she was interested in his work—he just hoped she'd find migration as fascinating as he did. "Before Perdecci," he said, "it was thought that, after orienting themselves to a compass direction, birds fly unthinkingly until they reach their destination. With no idea where they are from moment to moment."

"I'd bring up dating again—but I don't want to sidetrack you."

It was too late, he was getting sidetracked—starting to wonder about Valerie's instincts. But she seemed to want to hear about migration, and he got right to the heart of the matter. "Perdecci conducted this experiment in '64," he said. "He captured some Swedish starlings in Holland. The birds were on their way to their wintering territory in Brittany, southwest of there. He put them in covered cages and took them to Switzerland, where he released them. Now, if they were simply following an instinctually determined direction, they should have flown southwest to Spain. But they traveled north-by-west and turned up where they belonged, in Brittany."

"So somehow they knew . . ."

"Exactly. Where they were on the earth's surface. And without any visual cues—remember, they were transported in covered cages. They also understood their relationship to their destination. Like they had a built-in geo-positioning system."

"That's really beautiful."

"I guess it is. But you can imagine how it shook up the migration community. All the researchers started testing birds' sensitivity to wind currents, changes in the ionization of the atmosphere, magnetic isotherms. They'd blindfold them, put frosted contact lenses on them, strap magnets on their heads. Sometimes they'd even mutilate them—remove their pineal glands, severe the optic nerve, or destroy the inner ear."

Valerie recoiled. "Those birds needed a lawyer," she said as the waitress approached with their dinners—sole for her, flounder for him.

"Fortunately," Tanaki hastened to add, "we modern researchers have abandoned those methods in favor of observing the animals in their normal condition."

She commented approvingly and Tanaki picked up his narrative. "There was something about the data I couldn't walk away from. The idea that these birds—with their little bird brains—could figure out based on magnetic fields, or celestial soundings, or the ever-changing ionization of the atmosphere, their exact position, then calculate a vector to their destination, that amazed me." He settled for a moment to cut up the flounder. "I guess in a way, it was like those trout. I couldn't understand why these animals were behaving the way they did, and that bothered me, not being able to understand. It was like an alienation, it's hard to explain."

"I think I understand."

"I buried myself in migration studies. I figured if I learned everything there was to know about the subject, the answers had to reveal themselves. I spent most of the evenings of my junior and senior years in the library, studying everything from whales to aphids, or sitting up calculating energy requirements of long-distance migrants. You know, metabolism of stored fats and that kind of thing."

"It sounds like it could have been lonely."

"I guess it was," he replied, putting down his fork. "But I can't say I suffered any lasting damage. I was like an insect that spends part of its life in a cocoon, preparing for its next metamorphosis."

"And when the metamorphosis came? Did you turn into some strange and beautiful creature?"

"Just what you're seeing here. More strange than beautiful, I'm sure." She smiled indulgently while he organized his thoughts. "I've had some papers published," he said, "a couple of temporary teaching posts. A few research grants before this one. I guess the typical thing would be a tenured teaching job." He looked off, making some calculation. "I've put in some applications, but never really pushed. The only constant over the years has been migration."

Valerie grew thoughtful, then looked at the stars growing out of the darkening sky. "I can see how you got hooked on migration studies," she said. "But I sense something missing, some crucial element . . ."

"What do you mean?"

"*Cherchez la femme* is how the French say it, I believe," she said.

"A woman . . ."

"Mixed up in all this. How are my instincts?"

To his display of reticence she responded "Now don't get shy on me. After all, you've seen the heart on my sleeve . . ."

It was true, and he perceived a strength in her forthrightness. He took up his napkin and looked at it, searching for something. "There was one woman who was—I guess you could say—mixed up in all this. We worked together when I was in Europe."

"Of course. But will she remain nameless?"

"No," he said, looking up with a muted smile. "Her name's Ana. But I used to call her Bluebird."

"That's cute. She didn't mind?"

"Aside from when I first got to know her, I never called her anything else."

"Like the bluebird of happiness."

"I don't know about that," he said, looking away. Then he rallied, wanting to dispel a blue note left by his remark. "Maybe it came from a sort of game we used to play. She might say, you're acting like a beluga whale during mating season. And I'd say something like, I can't help it, I feel like a blackpoll warbler in late November. That kind of thing. Maybe you had to be there— or be a biologist."

The waitress came to clear the table. Amid the clatter Tanaki succumbed to other memories of the Bluebird, how they'd meet in quiet Belgian towns, spend the night on a Zeeland beach wrapped in an old sleeping bag.

He didn't share his reminiscences with Valerie. Nor did he tell her about the waxwings, how they came so unexpectedly that eight-year-distant spring. The medieval Dutch considered the little passerines heralds of plague and disaster. Now they'd come in great clouds, scouring the ground and trees for anything edible. He'd rushed to pick up the Bluebird in Pannenburg's jeep, not considering for a moment missing an invasion, a rarity in the migration world. They careened down narrow country roads, searching for the flocks. When they found them swarming over a village near the coast, he jammed the brakes, and they jumped out with nets, cameras, and a cotton bag full of metal rings they intended to attach to as many of the birds as they could capture. The waxwings were in a state of great excitement, and as Tanaki and the Bluebird scampered about netting them, with groups of curious villagers looking on, something happened. The line between Tanaki and bird blurred until he wasn't sure who was capturing whom. At one point he stopped, breathless, and found himself looking into the Bluebird's face. She, too, was out of breath. There was a vacant savagery in her eyes that he knew mirrored his own state of mind. For a moment everything was different. Who were they? *What* were they?

Of course he didn't tell Valerie how that night they loved one another with rapture unlike anything he'd ever experienced. Tender and hungry at once, with a fluttering of wings.

As the waitress wrapped up her duties, Tanaki looked at Valerie with a peculiar sadness in his eyes. She smiled reassuringly, knowing he'd been far away, and where his thoughts had been. Night had fallen, spots of light bounced on the sound. She must have questioned why she hadn't stuck with migration. She steered the conversation back to science.

"What about Perdecci's mystery, the one you hoped to resolve by exploring the depths of migration? Have the answers revealed themselves?"

"Not yet," Tanaki replied.

"You're still collecting data," she said helpfully.

"Yes, but the scary part is—I'm not sure more data will do it."

Both of them were slightly beery, and it was natural to put their arms around one another for support as they walked to the motel. Valerie leaned her head against Tanaki's shoulder; he felt a thrill at the touch of her hair against his face. Once in the room they came together without any real deliberation. It had been a long dry spell for him, and he liked how she was patient, and let him take the time he needed to get it right.

They lay facing one another in the wee hours.

"There's this bird in Africa," he said. "It lives in the desert..."

Valerie ran her fingers through his hair. He lay back and continued dreamily.

"When the rains come, all of a sudden the desert blooms with all kinds of life."

"How nice."

"So these little birds—these black-faced sparrows—they begin mating within moments of the first showers, so when their chicks hatch they can nurture them on all the seeds and fruits and insects."

"That's almost romantic," she said drowsily, shifting onto her side and nuzzling into him. They lay quietly, breathing softly together, then drifted off to sleep.

Tanaki opened his eyes before dawn, feeling wide awake. He was surprised to see Valerie lying there, breathing heavily. He felt an incredible tenderness toward her; he would have enfolded her in a warm embrace except that she looked so peaceful in her sleep he didn't want to disturb her. Noting by the clock that sunrise was near, he decided to walk down to the surf—there was a chance the dolphins would be running. Moving quietly, he pulled on his pants and slipped into the flip-flops he'd left by the door. He thought of the Yamaguchis, removing his shoes when he visited at their apartment. That small ritual had imprinted itself upon his consciousness.

The air felt moist. He strode over the sand toward the water and sat cross-legged a few feet from the surf's highest mark. He tried to put last night into perspective and concluded only that he wasn't sure what to make of it. He thought of Valerie sleeping soundly in the motel room. The extensive vista made him feel expansive and adventurous; the sound of waves anchored him in the cool sand with a sensation of density. He recalled some lines of verse, the few that had made any impression on him in his obligatory college lit class:

*Once, far over the breakers*
*I caught a glimpse*
*Of a white bird*
*And fell in love*
*With this dream which obsesses me.*

*Swifter than hail*
*Lighter than a feather*
*A vague sorrow*
*Crossed my mind.*

For some reason he found himself trying to meditate like he'd seen the Yamaguchis doing. He closed his eyes. The plunging breakers pulled him away from his habitual concerns until he was aware of nothing but the sound of the surf and his own breath. He sat for awhile, for the first time in his life thinking nothing at all. Without warning he dropped into a deep void. When he opened his eyes the sky was lightening over the horizon. He felt emptied and light. Gulls wheeled overhead; sandpipers ran along the surf-line. There was someone fishing up the shore; a couple strolled in the sand.

He got up and walked across the beach, over the boardwalk and into town, then made the four or five blocks that separate the ocean from the sound. Everything was quiet. He walked along the Assowoman Bay until he came to the inlet, where he stood and watched the ocean surge past great stone seawalls. When he came back to the beach the sun was well above the horizon.

He went down to the water's edge and walked toward the motel. There were a few surfers floating in the offing waiting for something worth the trouble. The beach was strewn with trash. Gulls and terns were indiscriminately trying to feed on plastic bags, cellophane hotdog wrappers, and styrofoam cups. He tried shooing the birds away, but they scattered only to relocate further up the beach and continue pecking at the rubbish. He felt sickened. He began picking up trash while scaring off the birds, waving his arms and shushing loudly. When his hands were full he looked around for a receptacle, but the nearest trash cans were far away on the boardwalk. He watched a black-backed gull snatch at a waterlogged plastic bag sloshing in the foam and resolved to clean up the mess there and then. He trudged up to the trash can, deposited his handful of wrappers and cups, and returned to the ocean's edge to continue picking up refuse while vainly trying to frighten away the birds.

He didn't notice the sun moving overhead, or the growing crowds that began to cover the beach until their blankets made it difficult for him to continue. He'd likewise failed to think of Valerie. She'd woken around ten, and after patiently waiting more than an hour, was making her way toward the beach to look for him.

When she sighted him a few blocks from the motel, out near the surf, she wasn't sure what to think. He was in the process of lifting the blanket of an apparent stranger to look underneath for garbage. When she approached he looked at her dazedly, as if he'd been on a long journey in the wilderness, and hers was the first human face he'd seen in months. He had a large wad of trash in his left hand. Particles of sand and salt formed a crusty film across his jaw. She followed along as he walked toward a trash can on the boardwalk.

"This stuff can kill these birds!" he said. "I can't believe someone doesn't do something about it."

"They're supposed to clean up the beach every night."

"Supposed isn't going to help these gulls."

"It must have been an accidental spill or something."

He was turning toward the water. She watched him walk away. "Don't you want breakfast?"

He made a vague gesture and continued walking. She stood on the beach and watched awhile. His thoroughness was frightening. He went to each blanket, politely explained the problem, and asked the sunbathers in question if they wouldn't mind if he serviced the area. The sun rose higher and bore relentlessly down on the burning sand. Valerie returned to the room, where she changed into her suit and applied some sunscreen. She had breakfast, then spent the day on the beach, taking occasional dips and reading her report.

As the dinner hour approached, and shadows from buildings beyond the boardwalk began their slow invasion of the beach, successive groups of bathers retired from the waning light, allowing Tanaki to work unimpeded. He knew he'd been taken for a crank more than once but he didn't let that bother him. His species had trashed up the beach, and if no one else was going to take responsibility for cleaning it, that wouldn't deter *him* from setting things right. It wasn't until the last oblique rays skimmed the water's surface that Valerie persuaded him, not without some difficulty, that he'd done everything humanly possible. They loaded the car in silence. Finally he apologized for not having been much of a companion during the day.

"I hope you don't think I'm losing it," he said.

"No, not losing it," she replied.

He didn't ask more questions, and they hardly spoke on the drive to Cambridge. Tanaki wondered about the events of the day—and what Valerie was thinking. Clearly something unusual had taken hold of him. He was reminded of his experience at the Baltimore conference when, at the end of his lecture, his mind locked up. He was a little worried about himself. Valere's face betrayed scant emotion as she listened to the pop tunes that monotonously followed one another on the radio, an endless saga of love and despair. When they pulled up under the big magnolias, she reached over the console and gave him a perfunctory hug. He said he'd call as he pulled his bag from the back and pushed the door shut.

# 9

# *Reynolds*

Reynolds possessed a knowledge of the bay that Tanaki, in spite of his prodigious scientific investigations, would never share. He'd come from a long line of oyster tongers and crab catchers; his ancestors had lived around the estuary for a score of generations; he'd imbibed a sense of the life in its waters with his mother's milk. While Tanaki could minutely describe the endocrinal functions going on inside some mollusk, he turned to Reynolds when he wanted to know where the best place to find oyster spat might be, or how to bait a crab pot. In fact, Reynolds' knowledge of the marine resources of the Chesapeake was nothing short of encyclopedic. He was instinctively aware of when certain fish species would be running, and where to locate them.

"They're a tasty fish, but you have to know how to fix 'em. They have this big bone you can't eat, and you have to know how to get that bone out. A lot of people say they're too bony, but that's because they don't know how to debone them. The trick is starting it right. You have to get ahold of this piece near the tail, then it'll lift right out."

As time went by, Tanaki also came to appreciate the older man's advanced understanding of the human animal. Though Reynolds was a past master at steering clear of the Center's politics, his habits of observation, long practiced on the water, and the propensity of the Center's staff to confide in him, left him unaware of little that went on at the station. One bright day a frustrated Tanaki approached him on the docks. "I can't believe this," he said, flourishing a boat request form. "He's done it again."

"No trip down to Tangiers, I suppose."

Tanaki didn't respond, but made a turn on the dock, looking out on the bay as if seeking an answer from its silent surging. "Has it always been like this?

"Oh no," Reynolds said. "Only since Guy came on board— just before you got here. Before that things made sense, for the most part anyway. Now every scientist on staff's been fouled up one way or another. And there doesn't seem to be much rhyme or reason to it."

"He claims he's following Coast Guard guidelines," Tanaki said without conviction.

Reynolds took a deep breath of bay air before revealing the depth of his skepticism. "That's the official explanation. Let me tell you something I've learned over the years. Usually the official explanation is to hide the facts, not reveal them."

"But why would he mess with our research?"

"I don't have a clue," Reynolds said, "but if you ask me, something's not cool."

Over the course of several trips in and around the bay the two men developed a simple division of labor, with the scientist in a pitch of investigative intensity, while Reynolds took care of practical matters like logistics, and helping Tanaki find what he was looking for. One thing Reynolds never worried about, however, was getting back to the Center. Ever since their first outing in the marshes, Tanaki had continued to impress him with an uncanny sense of direction—to the extent that the native son surrendered to an unquestioning faith in the pathfinding abilities of the newcomer.

They'd often stop for meals or, as the approaching solstice

brought a stronger sun, for cold drinks at a dockside market. At every stop Reynolds was hailed by old acquaintances, retired watermen with time on their hands, time to linger and chat with the proprietor or their buddies, waiting to see who or what might happen along.

Mid-morning. Tanaki stood on the shaded porch of Frank's Market, waiting for Reynolds, who'd gone around back to wash up. Buzz Richardson, a stout man of about sixty years, with spotty white stubble covering his fleshy face and wisps of fine hair lying across a blotchy scalp, stood beside him, leaning on a cane for support.

"So how's everything?" Buzz asked, looking straight out at the dock.

"Going pretty well," Tanaki said, popping the tab of a soda. "What about you?"

"Oh, fair to middling. And Johnny, how's he seem these days?"

Tanaki wondered why he didn't ask Reynolds himself. "Seems fine to me," he replied.

"Everything normal then?"

Tanaki thought he knew what Buzz was driving at. "Since you mention it, something funny happened a while back."

"Some kind of a spell?"

"Something like that. I figured it was probably too much sun."

"Sun—naw," Buzz said. "I've stood beside the man in the height of the summer's strength for more hours than I can tell you, pulling oysters in. I think it's that old war injury."

"I heard he was in the war."

"Never saw him falter for many a year. Then, a little before he retired, he started having these spells, just every now and then. Like he wasn't all there, you know. I figured it might have been that injury coming back on him somehow. I told him he should get it checked out, but he just wouldn't go to a doctor. I even called over to Shirley, but she couldn't get him to the doc either.

I guess the man just don't like docs."

Reynolds was approaching. "Smells like a thunderstorm," Buzz said loud enough for him to hear. "Ya'll better be careful out there."

The day was sultry, otherwise there was no sign of the storm Buzz prophesied in the baby blue sky full of fluffy cumuli. Dragonflies darted through the air and skimmers leapt over the surface of oil-brown water. Tanaki was sorting through a hunk of vegetation he'd just pulled up. He could see Reynolds, out the corner of his eye, standing in the aft of the skiff, surveying the marsh with a fathomless expression on his face. He was having a hard time concentrating—he couldn't get Buzz's remarks out of his mind. He'd grown to like Reynolds, and it dragged on him that his friend might be suffering from some disorder that could be treated, if he could be encouraged to seek help. He hated to bring up the fainting spell, concerned it might embarrass him. After some thought he decided on an oblique approach.

"I understand you were in the war," he said, his voice cutting through the marsh with a new, sad music.

"*The* war," Reynolds replied, turning his head slightly to acknowledge the remark.

"You mind my asking about it?"

Reynolds sighed as he turned, then sat on the bench that ran along the back of the skiff. "Not really," he said. "You know, it seems so long ago, in some ways, then, in other ways, like it was yesterday." He settled into the bench and collected himself a moment.

"It was like this," he said finally, wiping his brow. "I had this old friend Boots. We were working in a cannery up in Cambridge. Life was rough around here for us blacks. They were still lynching people, can you imagine? I'll never forget what happened to poor George Armwood. My folks knew him. And the people who did it just walked. One day I'm on break, and Boots comes up with this newspaper, a Negro paper he picked up over in Baltimore—he was always over there catting around on Saturday night. It's got a big advertisement saying we ought to enlist. The slogan, you know, they always gotta have a slogan, it was Double Victory. Double Victory, it says, end fascism abroad and racism at home. Sounded like a lot of victory, know what I mean? Boots looks at me and says, let's sign up.

"Now I'm thinking, I never really planned on being a soldier. I was just a farm boy and a fishing boy and now I'm working for the man at the cannery. It wasn't much of a job, but I had my gal—Shirley and me were already steady—and we were planning to get hitched. There were plenty of things that weren't cool, but I guess I was trying to ignore them. You couldn't cross Race Street without getting your butt jumped by a bunch of thugs, and the cannery foreman was always on us just because he could, because we were Negroes. So I say to Boots, what, fight a white man's war? What'd you rather do, he says, hang around here the rest of your life working jobs whites don't want for half the pay? I say, listen Boots, you really think anything's gonna change? I don't know, he says, but anything's gotta be better than yes-sirrin' the cannery foreman all day long. I say we could get killed over there. Yeah, he says, and on the other hand, having that nice warm rifle in our hands might make us feel like something more than second-class citizens.

"I told him he was crazy, but that night I couldn't sleep for thinking about what he said. I realized I was sick of the life I'd been living, and I couldn't see how I was going to spend the rest of my life the same way. I started thinking on Shirley. How am I gonna look her in the eye when I come home from work, after kissing some man's behind all day just because his skin's a different shade than mine? The more I thought about it the more troubled I was feeling. Sleep was out of the question. I got up and turned on the radio, quiet so as not to wake anybody, put my ear right up to it. It so happened they were talking about this book Hitler wrote, where he had a plan to put us back in slavery. That did it. I figured if I couldn't fight it on the Eastern Shore I could fight it somewhere else. A couple days later, there I am at the station with Boots, bound for Fort McClellan, Alabama."

He stood up and poled the skiff away from a hummock it was knocking against. He spent a moment looking over the marsh before sitting down again.

"Of course being in uniform didn't change much," he said with subdued laughter in his voice. "That shouldn't a been any surprise. We were in colored units. Course the officers were white. If we went off base—even in uniform—we couldn't so much as get a soda at a market. Soldiers were being treated so bad the army almost had a mutiny on its hands. I wasn't seeing any double victory, if you know what I mean. Not even a single victory. I was glad when they rushed us out to our staging bases on the West Coast."

They sat in silence, the midday sun pressing on their faces. They knew the story had to continue. Finally Tanaki spoke, close to a whisper.

"You were heading overseas."

Reynolds looked into the bottom of the boat, ran his hand across his head, seemed to twitch once or twice.

"Sure you don't mind talking about it?"

"It's not a problem," Reynolds said, staring hard into the boat's bottom. "My unit was in the Pacific. It was after Guadalcanal. We were taking back a lot of little islands. The Japanese were dug in pretty good. It was a bitch clearing those bunkers."

He stopped, like he'd end the story there. He took hold of the pole and made to stand up, then settled back onto the bench.

"I ran into a mortar shell and was evacuated to Hawaii. I sat out the rest of the war recovering." Now he got up for real and pushed with the pole. "What say we get some lunch?"

Tanaki assented, taking up a paddle and joining Reynolds in moving the skiff along. After a moment he broke their silence. "Whatever happened to the double victory?" he asked.

"Well," Reynolds said, "we beat the fascists, as you know."

"What about the other part?"

Reynolds slackened his poling. "Things didn't change overnight," he said. "You might say the Eastern Shore was still the Eastern Shore, America was still America. Maybe the change was more in me than the folks around me. You see, when I came back after spending eight months in that hospital, I was a different man. I figured Boots and I put ourselves on the line for the double victory. I wasn't about to let some ignorant racist mess it up. And then me and Shirley had gotten hitched and Louis was on the way. When I thought about him growing up in the world I was living in I couldn't figure it."

"I don't suppose you went back to work at the cannery."

"No," Reynolds replied with palpable satisfaction. "I didn't want to be cooped up anymore. I started working on the water. And what do you know, people got on easier out here. Seems there was more respect. It's like being on the bay made everybody a little more human, I don't know. All us watermen were struggling to make a living, black or white. I guess you could say we were in the same boat. Well, maybe different boats—but we'd work the same oyster bar, side by side.

"Of course there was still plenty of racism on the Shore. I had to deal with it all the time, still have to. But I had that new attitude. Maybe Boots was right about having that gun in my hands, I don't know. I just quit accepting it. Eventually, little by little, things started to change. A lot of other blacks were sick of the routine. Some whites too. We had a real time of it in the sixties, when H. Rap came out. I was in a few of those struggles. Yeah,

I've definitely smelled some tear gas in my time."

He poled steadily, composing his face as he drew in the clean air of the marsh in deep, steady breaths.

"Whatever became of Boots?" Tanaki asked.

"Boots," Reynolds started, his body stiffening, the skiff gliding aimlessly as he let the pole go loose. He glanced down long enough to say "Boots didn't make it back," then, breaking off his remark, lifted his head and resumed directing the little craft. Tanaki didn't turn around, but sensed his momentary distance, felt the skiff drifting. Then, as Reynolds regained his form, working his arms into the pole, Tanaki worked his paddle and felt the skiff skimming along at a good pace.

As they boarded the motorboat for lunch Reynolds spoke out of the blue.

"I got to tell you," he said, putting his arm around Tanaki's shoulders, "this war business ain't no picnic. But there are probably a few things worth fighting for. Just make sure you choose your battles carefully. Alright?"

Tanaki couldn't imagine why he might need the advice but Reynolds' embrace felt so fatherly he couldn't argue. "Sure," he said. "I'll do that."

# 10

# *The eel*

No one could say precisely when Tanaki's fascination with the eel began, though it must have been sometime after the ospreys nested, because he'd been too busy with the raptors to think about much else, and not much later than the bluefish runs, for he would shortly be caught up with a brilliant horde of Monarch butterflies. The American eel—*anguilla rostrata*—is the only truly catadromous fish in the estuary, spending its adult life in the bay and its tributaries, returning to the open ocean to spawn. Though the most numerous species in the watershed, present in every river and stream, *anguilla* is virtually unknown to most of the human denizens of the bay region. With its murky-yellow to mud-brown skin, and its propensity to burrow into bottom muck during the day, emerging to feed only under the cover of darkness, it happily remains a non-entity to millions of suburbanites who reside in the bedroom communities surrounding Washington and Baltimore.

Its breeding rites, which Tanaki thought heroic, might be considered ghoulish by those with less appetite for nature's mysteries. *Anguilla rostrata* spawns only once in a lifetime, its dramatic ritual of regeneration marking the end of its life. Biologists still don't know how an eel decides when its hour has come, and the age of spawning seems to vary wildly. On this score as on others, the eel has kept its reasons to itself. But on a dark November night, with the moon in first quarter, in the wake of an autumn storm, countless *anguilla* move stealthily downstream, aided by the prevailing currents in an inexorable procession toward the sea.

Biologists for many years were at a loss to describe the trajectory of spawning *anguilla* once they reach the Atlantic. It was clear they mate somewhere in the great deep, as the larval phase of the creature—like small, glassy willow leaves—had been identified as early as the nineteenth century floating in the Strait of Messina. But the location of the spawning rites remained as much an enigma to early twentieth-century biologists as it had to the ancients, who subscribed to the theory that eels spontaneously generate from river slime. In 1920 the Danish government commissioned the otherwise obscure biologist Johannes Schmidt to explore the matter. For years Schmidt's trawlers scoured the Atlantic, from Newfoundland to the Orkneys, from the Straits of Gilbraltor to the Antilles, dragging nets of a mesh fine enough to entrap the larvae. The searching vessels finally converged on the algae-mantled Sargasso Sea, their nets rendering growing numbers of ever-smaller larvae until it became clear that the provenance of the elusive animal had been discovered. Further investigation determined that after reaching the surface from deep spawning grounds, the larvae float effortlessly, unhurriedly, on the clockwise currents that wash both shores of the Atlantic, until arriving at the mouth of a suitable estuary. Having by now matured into small eels know as elvers, they swim up-current to their future homes in the stream or tributary where they'll nourish themselves and grow, living unobtrusively until they feel the urge to return again to the sea.

In spite of the progress that had been made, by the time Tanaki began his career, in clarifying the life history of *anguilla rostrata*, there remained one great mystery concerning the animal. Though it was clear that eels spawn under the Sargasso Sea, researchers remained frustrated in their attempts to locate an adult *anguilla* in open ocean, leaving a gaping lacuna in their understanding of the eel's spawning migration. It was certain that eels swim to their spawning grounds at very great depths, the only way to explain their having avoided capture over so many centuries. It was equally clear that spawning eels never return to their home streams, but die under the Sargasso Sea—this evident by the physiological changes undergone prior to migration, a process by which, for all practical purposes, a freshwater fish becomes a deep sea breeding machine. Its eyes bulge to twice their normal size, enabling it to see through the low levels of light at the great depths through which it will travel; the air bladder toughens; even the shape of the skull alters to withstand the tremendous pressures experienced in the abyss; and the muddy brown skin metamorphoses into shifting bronzed planes of pinks, greens and purples. The eel's normal coating of slime thickens as a prophylactic against the salty waters it must traverse, and the animal eats enormously, taking on great deposits of stored fat.

As the hour of departure nears the eel's digestive tract atrophies; once the spawning migration is underway the animal will not eat again. From this moment forward, all of its biological processes are geared to one thing and one thing alone. So imperative is the eel's procreative urge, kept in abeyance for a lifetime, that the animal will now sacrifice everything to its fulfillment. Tanaki verified the metabolic equations, satisfying himself that by the time the spawning eel reaches the Sargasso Sea, it will be emaciated, bones and tissues disintegrating, with no remaining energy reserves. Then, in a final spasm of excitement, surrounded by millions of its own kind both male and female, the animal will release its precious cargo of milt or spawn, adding to the misty stew from which the next generation will arise, before sinking quietly to the bottom to die.

A biologist who could locate an adult eel in open ocean would register a coup that, if not equaling Perdecci's, would be considered in the same class. But Tanaki had his own reasons, beyond professional glory, for his fascination with the eel. Its unobtrusive behavior through the years of its freshwater existence, thriving under our noses without our knowledge; its secure intuition in sensing its hour of departure; its tremendous bravery, setting out on its final mission through *mare incognita*; and its last burst of ecstasy under a vegetation-shrouded sea—all appealed to him greatly. Yet it must be conceded that as his thoughts became increasingly fixed on the object of following a migrating spawner beyond the continental shelf, he couldn't help but entertain an occasional fantasy about the astonished acclaim that would accrue if he could pull it off.

The morning the telemetry system arrived, he rushed to the shipping room to find Reynolds standing over an open box, staring with admiration at some shiny new devices he'd just liberated from their plastic wrappings.

"This is some beautiful equipment you got here," Reynolds said.

"Ever seen anything like it?" Tanaki asked, lifting a receiver out of the box.

"You kidding?" Reynolds exclaimed, straightening into military attention, "you're looking at Radio-Specialist-First-Class-John-D-Reynolds, United-States Ar—mee-sir!"

"I didn't know you worked with radios," Tanaki said, handing him the receiver.

"You didn't ask," Reynolds responded, running his fingers along the smooth metal casement. "Of course the devices we had in WWII were crude compared to this. This is beautiful stuff!"

"I hope it's beautiful enough to do the job."

"What's that?"

"Tracking an eel in open ocean."

"That could be a problem," Reynolds said.

"How do you see it?"

"The first thing is losing your signal. From what I hear, eels swim real deep once they hit the ocean. A radio signal attenuates pretty bad in salt water."

"That's why we're using acoustic telemetry. It uses sound waves. And they're having pretty good luck with it."

Reynolds raised an eyebrow.

"I know we're pushing the envelope, but I'm hoping it'll be good enough."

"Probably worth a try. You think an eel can carry this weight?"

"I don't know," Tanaki said. "My research tells me it'll take a lot to stop one of these guys once they decide to spawn."

"Sounds like us humans."

"Maybe even worse. They're very tenacious. There's a story in the literature about a plumber. Gets a call for a clogged drain in a thirteenth floor Manhattan apartment. He comes and takes the pipe apart. What does he find?—*anguilla rostrata*."

"Amazing," Reynolds said, turning the receiver this way and that, examining it from every angle.

"They've come a long way with this gear in the last few years," Tanaki said. "The transmitters we had over in Europe, they didn't have anywhere near this kind of range. I remember following a herd of swans through France once—damn, what a riot. My friend was with me. She was observing them with a pair of binoculars. I was driving. We were on these winding country roads, and of course the birds didn't have to follow the roads! If you let them get too far away they were gone for good."

"That's the way it goes sometimes, isn't it," Reynolds said absently, still absorbed in his examination of the electronics.

"Now with satellites, it looks like we're on the verge of following animals anywhere, right from the comfort of the lab."

"You don't say," Reynolds said, turning his attention from the receiver.

"It'd be a lot more efficient," Tanaki conceded, adding wistfully, "Probably take some of the fun out of it though."

Reynolds carefully laid the receiver in the box. "I suppose you had some fun with that friend of yours."

"I suppose we did," Tanaki replied, removing his glasses, pulling his shirt tail out to wipe the lenses.

Reynolds placed a hand on his shoulder. "Listen Dave, don't worry about a thing. I'm gonna take a good look at this gear and test it out thoroughly."

Tanaki stiffened. "Sure you know what you're doing?"

Reynolds pulled back in amazement. "Know what I'm doing? Davy, just leave this to me—we'll find that eel!"

Reynolds set out at once to make good his assertion, spending every minute for the next two weeks, when he wasn't out on the water, going over the technical manuals that came with the equipment. He showed up one morning with some tattered books, bound in Army green, that he'd used in the service. He was determined not merely to master the equipment but to improve it.

"Dave," he said one morning, "I'm gonna have to rebuild these hydrophones."

Tanaki masked his apprehension. But that evening, when he found Reynolds in the shop, standing over the costly devices with a soldering iron, his eyes betrayed his fears.

"Don't worry, Dave," Reynolds said, "When I finish with these things that eel can swim to Timbuktu and we'll find it."

Thus a strange troika came into being: Tanaki, whose ancestors crossed the Pacific to Hawaii and California; Reynolds, whose more remote predecessors migrated involuntarily across the Atlantic in the cramped and stinking hold of a slaver; and *anguilla rostrata*, seemingly oblivious to the commotion its ancient and inevitable migratory cycle was causing in a couple of human minds. Reynolds would have until autumn to work his electronic wizardry, then he and Tanaki would attempt to capture one of the spawners prior to its journey toward open ocean. They would affix the transmitter and attempt to follow in the Center's ocean cruiser—hoping finally to retrieve the defunct specimen over the Sargasso Sea after a flotation device delivered it to the surface.

# 11

# O-bon

Tanaki's acquaintance with the Yamaguchis had advanced considerably by the time the tidewater summer began inflicting its oppressive humidity upon Cambridge. On the sporadic occasions when he left the Center at a reasonable hour, they'd have him to dinner, after which the three of them would take advantage of the cooler air of evening to walk through the elm-lined streets of their neighborhood, or sit on the porch talking into the night. From the porch there was a clear view to the river at the end of Talbot Street, and when there was a moon you could see a silver gleam on the water.

The sisters virtually adopted him. They spoiled him unabashedly, explaining that he was the brother they'd always wanted. And Tanaki sensed at times, if it wasn't his vanity running away with him, another element, a competition for his attentions that wasn't strictly familial. Worlds apart in character and personality, they seemed to belong inextricably together, like different facets of the same gemstone. He wondered if it would be possible for a man to fall in love with only one of them. One day, he figured, they might have to resort to polygamy.

One thing that intrigued, perplexed, and even exasperated him, was a sense of unshakable calm about both of them, what seemed an inner satisfaction of sorts. He wasn't sure what to attribute it to—their being women, their close relationship, or something in their family upbringing or culture. Maybe it involved being heiresses to a substantial fortune, a luxury he was sure he'd never have to contend with.

Or perhaps it had to do with their peculiar religion, as it seemed to permeate their lives in a subtle, yet unmistakable fashion. Gleaning information from late-night conversations, Tanaki discovered there was a good deal more to the shrimp religion than Setsuko's first skeletal description had indicated. Its founder Ato was, by any measure, an exceptional character. After the death of his father, he not only prayed to the *kami* but, loin-cloth-clad, fasted for weeks on a windy headland in the dead of winter, convinced of the need for what he called a "sincere act of rectification." He became punctilious in the observance of the traditional rites, never failing to honor the *kami* at the appointed times, and applied himself to his work in the fishing fleet with an uncanny vigor, giving everything he had for no reason other than a willingness to serve. When his own business prospered he donated the profits to the rebuilding of temples. And as his religious movement gathered strength he earned notoriety by campaigning for a resolution for a national day of atonement for the violent excesses perpetrated under the country's militarist rulers before and during the late war.

Ato's doctrine was normally translated by the Yamaguchis as "pure action." He preached that the chief impediment to living well consisted of fear of the future, or what he called *what-might-happen* thinking, such as working to achieve economic security, for fear of *what-might-happen* if one were to follow one's inner springs of passion; or on the national level, adopting a bellicose stance in foreign affairs for fear of *what-might-happen* if a conciliatory policy were pursued. For Ato, the only activity worthy of one's energies was that which was purely spontaneous, growing out of one's inmost nature, guided through regular communion with the *kami* and a sense of connection to all beings. As to work, he maintained that it should be undertaken not out of fear of penury, but as a joyous sharing of one's best gifts, just as nature, buddhas, and ancestors bestowed their gifts without expecting recompense. *What-might-happen* thinking, Ato counseled, leads to emotional and spiritual blockage, and if not checked in time, entrains personal and collective disaster.

In the sixties, Ato once again plunged into the civic arena, spearheading a fight to protect the natural world, imbued as it was, for him and his followers, with the spirit of *kami*. Relying, as he had done before, on a sincere act of rectification, he conducted hunger strikes to stem the decimation of whale populations, and to convince big fishing concerns to take measures to protect dolphins from needless slaughter in their nets. Though these rigors didn't achieve their goals, and may have hastened his death in the seventies, his movement carried on without him. Yamaguchi père, Tanaki had learned, was now a prominent, if not popular, spokesman for more stringent regulation of ocean harvesting.

It was a warm Saturday night. Tanaki had spent most of the day at the refuge. He made a point of getting back before dark. Setsuko had said that she and Nariko had plans for him that evening. The idea of polygamy didn't cross his mind. At least not much.

He'd no sooner stepped into his apartment than there was a knock at the door. It was Nariko. "Sorry to bother you . . . too soon," she began. "It's . . . almost time to start."

"No problem, Nari. What is it we're going to start, anyway?"

"I can't . . . explain now. Setsuko said don't . . . waste time. You know she gets a little . . . anal—is that the right word?"

Tanaki chuckled at Nariko's growing familiarity with the

subtleties of character description in English. He went to the bathroom and splashed cold water on his face. After brushing his teeth and changing into fresh clothes he headed downstairs.

When he stepped onto the porch he was greeted by a vision of the Yamaguchi sisters in traditional Japanese kimonos. Setsuko had been more painstaking in her approach, right down to the traditional makeup, whereas Nariko's costume left the impression of, not a studied deshabille, but a hurried effort at meeting the requirements of the occasion. At first the delicate refinement of the shimmering silk garments seemed glaringly out of place on Talbot Street. But as the three friends stepped off the porch and walked down the sidewalk toward the river, the sisters radiated a transcendent beauty that suffused their surroundings, finding an echo in every feature of the townscape.

They led Tanaki toward the small harbor where Cambridge Creek debouches into the Choptank, the minor embayment that was the locus of the community in colonial times. Their destination was the Chesapeake headquarters of Yamaguchi Enterprises, a large, hangar-like structure of corrugated metal extending over the harbor. After walking alongside the building on a boardwalk they entered the small front office. Tanaki's first impression was a powerful odor of fish. The sisters proceeded through the office and passed through a door on its back wall. This brought them into a cavernous space that was half-terrestrial, half-marine. The floor, composed of the same planking used on the outdoor piers and walkways, didn't extend over the entire area of the enclosure, but terminated at steel railings, exposing the waters of the harbor. Here, Yamaguchi ships could enter and unload their catch.

Nariko, with apparent pride, pointed out a placard hanging over the office door. It bore the company credo which, she informed Tanaki, was chanted *en masse* by Yamaguchi employees before beginning each day's work. She began to recite it out loud, and Tanaki joined in with playful solemnity:

*We are grateful to the people of the world*
*We will not forget that our fleet exists for the sake of our customers.*
*Sharing good times and bad, we will cooperate*
*And not forget to encourage one another.*
*Setting aside the past and worries for tomorrow,*
*We will find our joy in the task set before us today.*
*Remembering that all beings are precious*
*We resolve to be good stewards of the earth.*
*And we will not fail to show our gratitude*
*To the ancestors and the kami*
*For all we have and will receive.*

Nariko squeezed Tanaki's arm in delighted recognition of their moment of camaraderie, then pointed out, down one of the building's long walls, a shrine of rich, dark wood. It housed a larger-than-life image that Tanaki recognized from the print in the Yamaguchi's apartment as the god Ebisu.

He followed Nariko and Setsuko to a corner where a large number of paper lanterns had been stockpiled. He watched them place them in shallow baskets of exquisite workmanship. It was only after he helped carry the lanterns onto the landing, and the three friends sat relaxing on the thick planking, that Setsuko offered an explanation of what was going on.

"You don't know about *O-bon?*" she asked incredulously.

"I think my mother told me something about it once."

"Is that all?" Setsuko asked.

Tanaki turned his palms up and looked at her blankly. She exchanged a pitying glance with Nariko.

"Looks like some kind of party," he finally offered.

"Well, not exactly," Setsuko said, "but you're not entirely wrong. Sure you never honored your ancestors? Ever?"

"Well I guess I respect them . . . I don't know much about them, actually."

"These lanterns are called *toro*," she said, picking up one of the delicate boxes. "See the candle inside." She held up the lantern so he could see. "Now, little brother, pay attention!"

Tanaki scratched his head in jest. Nariko softly giggled. Setsuko sat the *toro* on the landing and addressed Tanaki more earnestly. "A couple of days ago Nariko and I placed some special offerings on the shrine. Flowers, sake, rice dumplings—Nari, am I forgetting anything?"

Nariko nodded in the negative.

"The offerings are a way of showing our respect and appreciation to all the people who made our lives possible."

A shrill chorus of frogs and insects swelled beyond the harbor.

"We also lit a *makaebi* fire to help the old ones find their way across the great divide. That's how we welcomed them back. For a little visit, to hang out for a couple of days."

Tanaki peered into the gathering dusk, wondering in spite of himself if they were out there somewhere.

"Tonight we're sending them home, back to the other side." Setsuko's kimono rustled as she began to stir. "These lanterns will light their way back."

The three friends crouched on the landing. A humid breeze washed over them, softly ruffling the paper of the *toro* as Setsuko arranged them in neat rows. After they were in order, Nariko knelt at the edge of the pier. Setsuko grasped one of the lanterns: she removed a box of wooden matches from the folds of her kimono, lit the small candle inside, and handed it to her sister. Bending toward the water, Nariko floated the glowing box on the surface, giving it a push away from the landing. The *toro* floated towards the river's channel, echoed by fireflies that hovered in the air. Setsuko lit another and passed it to Nariko, who sent it on its way after the first, and so on, until an ethereal parade of luminous points extended into the Choptank.

Darkness had fallen.

"You know," Setsuko said, as the last of the lanterns made its way into the river, "it's interesting. Since *O-bon* welcomes ancestors back to their home towns, I'm really not sure whose ancestors we've been venerating."

"You mean . . ." Nariko began.

"I mean it's just possible we're honoring the ancestors of Cambridge, and not our own."

Nariko was thoughtful for a moment before responding, almost to herself, "Does it really matter?"

# 12

# Ancestors

Thoughts of the *O-bon* ceremony lingered in Tanaki's mind for days. The three friends danced at a local nightspot afterwards, the closest feasible substitute for the jubilant street parties that mark the close of the ceremony in Japan. But it was the quiet moments watching the *toro* drift into the river that penetrated Tanaki with an odd longing, a longing he identified with a desire, now intensified in remembrance, to dive in and follow the lanterns on toward the bay. He'd never thought much about ancestors before—his or anyone else's. "How ironic," Setsuko had said, forcing her voice over the loud music at the Happy Clam Bar and Grill. "You, a migration specialist, never studied the migrations of your own ancestors. I'll bet your grandparents caused quite a stir when they left their villages for America." He countered that his parents had made no attempt to pass on what they knew of their antecedents. "My folks didn't even like discussing their own experiences in life," Tanaki explained. "I guess I've always thought that was normal."

But can someone live without a past beyond his own personal history? And if so, how? Tanaki had never pondered the question, absorbed, as he'd been throughout his life, in investigations of nature. But his simple participation in the *O-bon* ceremony awakened a dormant region of his being. He became preoccupied with the idea of the past. And he no longer found it possible, as he walked through the streets of his river-washed town, to think only of an assortment of services answering to the practical needs of David Tanaki—the dry cleaners, the diner, the bank, the post office, the drug store. Now every street, every old house, every quiet yard seemed haunted by the spirits of those who'd walked the streets, inhabited the houses, and sat quietly of a summer evening in yards full of birdsong and the scents of flowers. He pondered over Setsuko's last remarks on the landing of Yamaguchi Enterprises—about honoring the ancestors of Cambridge—and on a quiet Saturday morning walked to the town's library, a squat brick building near the courthouse. He addressed himself to the precise, motherly ladies who ran the place, and one of them directed him to a quirky assemblage of colonial history with a title that appealed to the biologist in him: *Albion's Spawn in the Great Shellfish Bay*.

His interest in any but the broadest strokes of history had been so perfunctory—a couple of required courses he'd looked upon as rude interruptions of his migration studies—that his encounter with Professor Huntley's tome had an effect upon his imagination similar to that which might have attended a voyage to some distant planet. There were the first European explorations, so poorly documented it's uncertain whether Verrazanno actually spotted the Virginia capes in 1524. Then the brief and fruitless attempt by Spanish Jesuits to settle the banks of the James River prior to the arrival of the English in 1607. The "starving time" at Jamestown, when the living dug up graves to devour the dead; when John Radcliffe, sent to the much-abused Indians for food, instead had the flesh scraped from his bones with seashells; when a crazed colonist ran through the marketplace crying there was no God, only to fall victim to the native inhabitants while hunting in the forest that day. There was the amazing Opechancanough (rumored to have been the young brave educated by remnants of the failed Jesuit mission) who after years of cagey

sparring with the better-armed colonists, master-minded the
bloody but futile attack of 1622. And a pitched battle involving
all of three vessels on the waters of the bay, settling once and for
all Lord Calvert's claim to jurisdiction over Kent Island.

Tanaki was entranced by the improbable characters that made
up the early history of the bay. But nothing intrigued him like
the story of Margaret and Mary Brent, two sisters who migrated
to the Chesapeake in the early years of the Maryland colony.
Reading about how they established their own household,
eschewing the protection of their brother Giles, he couldn't
escape an odd feeling that he knew them. He cheered when
Margaret displayed a genius for legal matters, representing herself in the kinds of land disputes likely in a time of poorly defined
property rights. He experienced a prideful satisfaction when she
began representing her neighbors as well, profiting so much from
parcels given in payment that she became one of the colony's
largest landholders. When she came to the attention of the governor, however, he felt an odd unease, a premonition of trouble.
Still, she became one of Leonard Calvert's closest advisors and
the executor of his will.

It seemed to Tanaki that her hardiness of character was never
displayed more clearly than on the occasion of Ingels' rebellion, a short-lived spin-off of the English Revolution. "After the
governor's supporters managed to drive Ingels and his Round-
heads from St. Mary's City," Huntley wrote, "a new crisis arose
when the governor found himself unable to pay the soldiers.
When these mutinied, threatening to take the city on their own
account, Margaret Brent stepped into the breach. After chastis-
ing the mutineers for their greed and disloyalty, she promised to
use her influence to see that they be paid, but not without threatening to take her cane to anyone still lingering on the parade
grounds after five minutes."

Tanaki would have preferred that the story end there, at the zenith of Margaret Brent's star. To have seen her retire happily on her estates, enjoying the prestige that was clearly her due after rendering such services to her neighbors and the colony. But she ran into trouble when the governor died. She was right to liquidate his properties to pay off his debts, but the Lord Proprietor—comfortably ensconced in England—didn't take the loss to the family's estate gently. In a letter by the first ship, he impugned her probity and relieved her of her duties.

Tanaki felt personally stung by the injustice. He stood up and made a couple of turns around the table. He didn't really want to know more, but the chapter was near its end. He sat down and continued reading.

"The governor closed his letter," Huntley wrote, "with a slighting reference to the lady's not-too-distant ancestors. 'This mortification,' wrote Calvert, 'might well be brought upon us by the spawn of a fishmonger.'"

"Fishmonger," Tanaki blurted, breaking into laughter. "Setsuko and Nariko!"

His feelings were somewhat assuaged by the episode's conclusion, describing how Margaret and Mary sold out and moved to Pennsylvania, where they enjoyed a bountiful retirement. While walking home, burdened with tomes on everything from the Underground Railroad to the development of the tobacco industry, he again thought of the Yamaguchis. "I wonder if they could run into problems with the authorities?" he asked himself. But he just as quickly dismissed the thought, hastening his pace as the magnolias' crowns came into view.

# 13

# *Haskel*

By mid-summer a new pattern was developing in Folker's meddling. He increasingly cloistered himself in his office, refusing calls or visitors. Interaction with staff was funneled through Cynthia, who made the rounds, distributing memos and communiqués. Sitting in his cubicle one afternoon with a freshly denied boat request in hand, Tanaki knew he needed a change of scene. He thought of Bob Haskel, a biologist he'd met at a professional meeting he'd recently attended at Folker's behest. Haskel had invited him to visit the Muddy Creek Wildlife Management Area to look into some intriguing research he was conducting with a network of committed scientists.

Haskel and his colleagues were working to address the displacement of waterfowl from their wetland habitats. Whether in the Central Valley of California, across the pothole country of the northern plains, or around the Chesapeake itself, everything from filling for agriculture and development, to fouling by pollutants, was creating profound disturbances in the life-cycles of animals Tanaki considered among the most noble on earth.

He arrived at Muddy Creek in a little over an hour. He pulled off the paved road onto a dirt drive that wound through the ubiquitous loblollies, hearing gravel crunching under the tires. He rolled up the window to close out the cloud of dust that rose from the wheels. At the end of the drive he entered a clearing.

A redwood house sat in the middle of a broad lawn. A considerable number—perhaps a hundred or more—of snow geese milled around in groups of ten or twenty.

He was parking the car to one side when Haskel emerged from the house, walking energetically across the front porch and onto the lawn. As he crossed the yard, excited geese surrounded him in a tight peloton, shadowing his every step. Soon the entire gaggle, Haskel included, were at the car, and Tanaki couldn't help but laugh as Haskel said hello, reaching over his honking charges to shake his hand.

"We'd better go inside," he said, "or we'll have no peace."

As they headed for the porch, sidestepping blotches of guano on the lawn, Haskel told Tanaki to go in through the front door and wait for him in the kitchen. "I'll meet you inside," he clipped in rapid staccato as he bolted around the side of the house, the geese setting off after him. Tanaki walked down a hallway to the rear of the house, entering the kitchen in time to see Haskel squeezing through the door, a flurry of white forms fluttering and flapping behind him. He snapped the door shut and calmly walked across the rough tile floor toward Tanaki. Clearly winded, he invited him to sit at the kitchen table, a pine plank affair on delicate iron legs.

"Okay," he said, a welcoming smile on his face, "where were we?"

Tanaki stared at him for a long moment, unable to dislodge the image of him edging through the door surrounded by crazed waterfowl. He was a man of fifty-some years, with short-cropped, reddish hair and a build that, while slight, was still taut. His gold-rimmed glasses had slid down his nose.

The geese were hopping around outside the kitchen, fluttering up to the windows and flapping their wings outrageously, trying to get Haskel's attention. Beyond them Tanaki made out a small aircraft parked in an open space behind the house.

"This must get distracting," he remarked.

"Just an over-heated mimetic instinct," Haskel said. "It's funny," he continued, looking toward the window, "I feel they know I'm their last, best chance." He watched silently for a moment, then turned back to Tanaki. "It's all part of the job."

"Maybe I shouldn't say this," Tanaki ventured. "I don't know you very well. But it seems these geese have made you a prisoner in your own house—I can't believe that's part of the job."

"You can't blame the geese," Haskel said. "After all, they probably think I'm their mother. Besides, I've got a soft spot right here for these silly birds." He patted his chest.

"I'm surprised to see them this time of year," Tanaki remarked. "Shouldn't they be up north breeding?"

"That's just it, they should be, but aren't. It's a long story, and not very edifying, but if you want it, here it is. This was one of the first groups I trained to follow my plane."

Tanaki leaned forward, straining to hear over the honking and flapping going on outside. Haskel raised his voice.

"They were HATCHED up in CANADA," he yelled. "But when the CANADIAN GOVERNMENT got wind that they were being used in experiments in the STATES, a big bureau-cratic FUSS ensued and they REFUSED to let me bring them back into the COUNTRY. So they're REFUGEES for the time being, and I'm all they've GOT until we sort this mess OUT."

"Good God," Tanaki said, "what do they expect, passports?"

Haskel gestured that he couldn't hear him. "We'd better relocate," he hollered.

He got up from the table and showed Tanaki to the family room. There were several photos, Haskel at various stages of his life with a woman and a couple of children. Tanaki bent down to examine one.

"The wife and kids," Haskel offered.

"Cute little ones," Tanaki said.

"That's an old photo," Haskel responded, picking up the framed image, looking at it tenderly. "The kids are in college now."

"What does your wife do?"

"Another long story. She's taking a break. Visiting friends and relatives, having a breather." Haskel's voice cracked, and Tanaki felt a little alarmed. But as they sat down, he gazed steadily at his bookcase, then spoke in measured tones as he turned toward Tanaki.

"You know," he said, "I sit here nights and think about the way we're living on this planet. Here we are, modern *homo sapiens*, the so-called wise hominid. And we've evolved, if that's the word for it, to the point where we can work our will on the biosphere. We can take care of it, or destroy it. And look what we're doing. We're in the middle of a mass extinction, on par with the pre-Cambrian die-out. And we're causing it. Us."

Tanaki shifted in his chair, not sure what to say. Haskel glanced toward the shimmering foliage of a maple outside the window. "Sometimes I think of the earth as a Rorscach blot on which we project our psyches," he said. "And I wonder, what kind of psyche would wish for all this death and destruction, this wanton plundering of life?"

His eyes now bore into Tanaki, who couldn't avoid a response. "I don't know what to say, Bob," was all he managed. "Don't you think there's any hope?"

"Oh, there's always hope," Haskel said in a lighter vein. "And I'm sorry. I don't mean to harangue you. Preaching to the choir, I'm sure. I'm just an old man who spends too much time alone." Flapping and honking noises drew his gaze to the windows, where geese were beginning to congregate.

He began to rise from his chair. "Yes, there's hope," he repeated. "But we'll have to be very strategic from here on out. There's nothing pristine out there anymore. It pains me to say it, but the time for preserving ecosystems is past. In the future we'll have to re-create them, if there's anything left to re-create them with. Meanwhile, we have to do what we can, even it's just rear-guard actions. That's all I'm doing with these geese. Keeping them temporarily safe. My next challenge is to find a viable breeding ground. After a test run, I'll see if I can induce larger flocks to join in as my colleagues and I find habitats for them. Admittedly, a lot of this depends on relatively untested theories on collective intelligence, like Rupert Shelldrake's work."

The entire gaggle were now creating an uproar at the windows of the family room. Haskel moved to the door, beckoning Tanaki to follow. He offered to show him around, and as the jeep made its way along the refuge road, a low-flying V cast its spreading shadow from above.


Back at the Center Tanaki told Reynolds about Haskel's geese.

"Snowbirds, you mean."

"No, I mean snow geese."

"Wait a minute. Big white goose with black wing tips?"

"Yeah, snow geese."

"Well, we used to call 'em snowbirds. When I was a kid our folks had us convinced those birds needed all kinds of help to keep flying. At the end of winter, when we'd see 'em in formation, or just hear 'em coming in the distance, we'd all run into the yard. My grandmother'd be saying, "Hurry, now, hurry! Those geese've got a long journey to make, and they need all the help they can get!" And we'd go running outside like we were crazy and all start hollering at the geese. "Come on, geese, don't stop. Come on, come on, you've got to keep flying."

"You know, it wasn't until I was in the service that it occurred to me that those geese probably didn't need our help to get where they were going."

He paused.

"They didn't, did they?"

He watched a moment as Tanaki tried to engineer an earnest response, then laughed gently as he patted him on the back.

# 14

# Melanie Kersey

Tanaki's visit to Haskel, while offering a day's relief from the Center's claustrophobic atmosphere, did little to solve his wider problem. The fact remained that his research was reaching a bottleneck—he had to get to those sites in the lower bay, where highly saline waters support ecosystems not found elsewhere in the estuary. He particularly wanted to explore the salt grass meadows that occupy large expanses of the lower shore.

*Zugenruhe*, that's what the German researcher Neuman named it. "Migratory fidgets," the tendency of caged birds to exhibit restlessness during migration season, fluttering their wings and hopping about, orienting themselves in the direction they'd fly were they able to execute their urge to move.

The phenomenon had been well studied. Researchers employed caged birds in attempts to determine the effects of photoperiodism, atmospheric pressure, and temperature on the onset of the migratory impulse, and whether the direction of the bird's orientation could be altered by the use of magnetic fields, or by exposing the animal to planetarium skies full of bogus celestial landmarks. Tanaki had taken part in a number of these studies; he'd always felt a certain pity for their subjects as he watched them hopping and flapping with the coming of evening, certain they knew they were missing a rendezvous with destiny without the means to do anything about it.

Now he'd become one of them.

Reynolds walked toward a dock where Tanaki sat in one of the station's motorboats. He was carrying a soda in each hand and shaking his head quizzically. As he stepped into the boat Tanaki asked what was going on.

"I was talking to some of my buddies in there, and it sounds like something's up. Some kind of demonstration or something, way down past Bristol."

"A demonstration," Tanaki said, "what's it about?"

"Hard to say," Reynolds replied. "All I could make out from the fellas inside was some hoopla about a bunch of bones," and he began humming, *dem bones, dem bones, dem dry bones* . . .

"Bones," Tanaki murmured, his scientific curiosity piqued. "Let's go down there and take a look."

Soon the faded red pickup rumbled over narrow McCaddam roads, with Reynolds, Tanaki, and Buzz Richardson pressed against one another on the springy seat of the hollow cab. With both windows open, the smell of chewing tobacco and fish mingled with the warm aroma exuded by the trees and moist earth alongside the road. Buzz was driving Reynolds and Tanaki down the peninsula in search of the altercation that was the main topic of conversation in Frank's Market when Reynolds stopped in for sodas.

"Wonder if it could be some old graves like they went and dug up over to St. Mary's not long ago," Buzz had said to no one in particular.

"Wasn't they looking for some of Calvert's people from way back in Colonial days," a portly man in overalls, leaning against the cooler, put in.

"Lord knows there's enough bones buried around here to keep a whole crew busy a couple a lifetimes," Buzz replied.

"Those folks sure made a fuss over digging up them graves though, didn't they," Frank chimed in from behind the counter. "You'd a thought they was digging up somebody's mother or something."

"Seems they just wanted to know whose bones they were, way I remember it."

"Never did find out, either," the man leaning on the cooler concluded.

As Buzz chatted with Reynolds and Tanaki he periodically stuck his head out the window to spit chaw juice on the road. His spirits were good. He'd agreed to drive them down the peninsula with eagerness. He and his comrades were relics of an era when hundreds of Eastern Shore men supported their families working on the bay's skipjacks, dredging for oysters that were once more plentiful in the Chesapeake than anywhere in the world. Now it was seldom that anyone asked him to do anything, and he was by nature a helpful sort. "By the sounds of it, down around Marsh Bay," he offered, pausing to spit.

"Anyways, somewhere near Sommerfield," Reynolds said, watching the breeze play in the passing pines.

"Good hour."

Tanaki sat squashed between the two larger men, watching sun glint on specks of rock in the pavement. Now and then a bird swooped down over the road, barely missing the truck's windshield. All around there was stillness, and in the afternoon heat he sensed the earth sweating. Passing cars were few and far between. The road was lined with forest, broken here and there by fields, or a house with a lone child playing in the yard, a dog panting on the porch.

In the cab conversation lagged. Lulled by the truck's movement, conscious only of the hum of the tires on the road, Tanaki didn't notice the commotion until Buzz applied the brakes. There were several police cars halfway off the road with emergency lights flashing. Four men in hard hats were speaking to a couple of cops, and off the road he could see construction equipment through a stand of pines.

Buzz pulled over. He and Reynolds swung open the doors and climbed out. Tanaki followed. They stepped stealthily through the grove, making their way toward the dull-yellow earth-moving machines that sat in a clearing about a hundred feet ahead. They heard loud voices and were able to make out several people on and around the machines by the bright colors of their clothing. When they got to the edge of the woods the scene began to make sense. The huge rigs sat amid piles of dirt that appeared to have been excavated from several gaping holes. A vaporous dust rose from the ground into the sultry air. The bay could be seen through the trees, not far off.

The people in the clearing wore T-shirts advertising their allegiance to the Nanticoke Indian Heritage Society. Otherwise Tanaki would have been hard-pressed to classify them as First Americans. They wore typical modern clothing, and their appearance varied from Mongoloid to Negroid and Caucasoid. Several carried large picket signs. There were about two dozen of them, not an impressive force. But they kept up a steady stream of commentary, one voice blending into another.

"Respect Native rights!"

"Leave the dead in peace!"

"Heritage over profits!"

"Save sacred spaces!"

"No more broken promises!"

Before Tanaki could process everything the cops began moving into the clearing. Several of the protesters lay on the ground before the rigs. Others draped their bodies over the machines' treads. When the officers came within earshot of the protesters a dark-haired young woman climbed onto the front-end of one of the dozers and addressed them sharply.

"These are our ancestors' graves. How'd you like it if we were digging up your grandma's bones?"

The officers stopped and squinted up at the diminutive figure silhouetted against the blazing sun. "Why don't you just come down like a nice little girl?" one of them said. "Nobody's gonna dig up anybody's grandmother."

"Bullshit!"

"Look, I hate to do this, but if you don't come down nice, you're going to come down not nice—know what I mean?"

She flipped him the bird.

A sergeant barked orders and the cops began moving among the protesters. The Nanticokes were obviously schooled in non-violent resistance. As the officers approached each of them, they let themselves be carried to the waiting squad cars without struggle. But the young woman remained defiant. As they carried away her comrades, she sat at the controls of the dozer with arms folded across her chest, dark shades masking her eyes, her jaw set. After finishing with her associates, the cops turned back to deal with her in force. Tanaki watched with keen attention. A phrase began going through his mind: *the nail that sticks up . . . the nail that sticks up . . . the nail that sticks up . . .*

He broke from the cover of the trees and dashed toward the bulldozer, dust spitting from his sneakers. The woman turned in amazement. When he reached the dozer he leapt without missing a step, planted a foot briefly on the tread and propelled himself onto the seat, landing with a thud that left a hollowness in his chest. Instinctively, remotely, he turned the key in the ignition and grabbed the most prominent looking lever. The cops hesitated as the grumbling dozer turned wildly on itself, first to one side, then the other. Tanaki struggled to master the controls.

"What on earth are you doing?" the protester screamed over the din of the engine.

"I don't know," he said, gritting his teeth in concentration.

He managed to swing the monster in a widening arc. The cops backed off. One grabbed a walkie-talkie.

"The boy's gone completely crazy," Reynolds said, wiping his brow with his handkerchief.

"Stop this thing, you maniac," the woman yelled. "You're going to get us killed."

Tanaki screwed up his face in consternation. "I don't know how!"

The dozer careened madly, bumping over mounds of earth that had been turned up in the excavation. Tanaki experimented with levers but accomplished nothing more than to cause the scoop to bang up and down willy-nilly, tilting and clanking. Just as a squadron of state troopers roared up, the machine pitched into a shallow trench and slammed to a stop, throwing Tanaki into the dirt, the young protestor against the control panel.

The cops ran to the grinding, smoking dozer. Two of them grabbed a shaken and dust-covered Tanaki while a third clambered onto the seat and stopped the machine. The woman, though not injured, was too rattled to put up any but the most ineffectual struggle as she was cuffed.

After booking, the cops released everyone except her and Tanaki, whom they charged with trespassing, resisting arrest, and assault on a peace officer. They were consigned to adjacent holding cells in the old county jailhouse. She sat on a bench staring straight ahead, still wearing dark shades. Tanaki stood in the middle of his cell trying to figure the whole thing out. "I'm sorry if I made things worse," he said. He looked at her, but she made no move to respond.

"I don't know what got into me."

She stared at the floor. He sat down. She turned calmly.

"What I don't get," she said, "is what the hell were you thinking?"

"That," he said, "is something I can't give you an answer to."

"Are you Indian?"

"No, I'm from Michigan."

As soon as the remark left his lips he realized it was idiotic.

"You're strange," she said.

She seemed to relax a little and leaned back, propping herself on one elbow. Tanaki's thoughts drifted to his own situation and how he was going to get out of it. He figured he was going to need a lawyer, and he only knew one—Valerie Stanton. But he didn't know if he should call her. He'd phoned a couple of times since Ocean City, but she'd seemed distant, and steered their conversations to environmental policy. When he'd brought up the possibility of getting together, she complained of a heavy workload and said she'd let him know. Maybe the trip to the beach didn't trip her trigger. But he thought he could at least say they were friends, and he was embarrassed at the thought of trying to explain himself to a complete stranger. Somehow he knew she'd cut him a break, help him without making him feel like a jerk. When a deputy came by he asked if he could make a call to Baltimore.

After the deputy returned him to his cell, he spoke to Melanie. "Say," he said, "I've got a friend coming down and she's a lawyer. Maybe she can get us out of here."

"And when will your *friend* be getting here?" she asked, raised eyebrows emerging above the rims of her shades.

"No, really," Tanaki chuckled, feeling on the defensive. "She's a friend." ("Hells bells," he thought, "she doesn't miss a thing!")

He walked aimlessly around the cell. Though he could feel her gaze, he tried to behave casually. It was quiet. They must have been the jail's only prisoners. He stopped in the middle of the cell and turned toward her.

"Were your grandmother's bones really dug up over there?"

"Why do you ask?"

"I was just concerned." He ambled to the window at the back of the cell, where he could see the day's last clouds floating by.

"You know," he said, "I've been doing some reading about the Shore. I've got to tell you, I find the history fascinating."

"I hope you're not reading that bull by Huntley they give out at the public library."

"Is there something wrong with the book by, who was it, Huntley?"

"Is there anything wrong with it? I mean, where have you been?"

He tried to suppress the pained expression that painted his face.

"Look," she continued, "I've seen worse. At least he mentions First Americans, in spite of his obsession with the ignorant con-quistadors who savaged my people and raped the land. Above average for a white man, I guess."

Tanaki needed to change the subject; he didn't have a dog in this fight but felt an unpleasant heat directed his way. "I suppose that was a cemetery down there."

"Cemetery's not the right word. That's not how my people did things."

She fell silent, fixing her gaze into the darkening cell. Tanaki stood chin in hand, waiting for more elaboration. His discomfort was barely manageable when she continued.

"There was a kind of hut—it was up on stilts—called a Chicisoan. You'd think it's gross."

"Don't worry about me. I've dissected every organism imag-inable."

"I guess that's one way to learn," she said, turning slightly toward him.

Tanaki didn't know how to respond. She faced forward again, seeming far away. Then she began meditatively. "They'd scrape the flesh off the bones with seashells. Wrap the bones in the skin. After awhile they'd pick the bones clean and bury them with the rest of the ancestors."

Tanaki approached the bars between the cells. He grabbed a

couple of them and leaned his weight against the cool metal. "So that was a mass grave over there."

He let the silence expand until it engulfed him. Then he spoke in self-defense, against the silence, against the bars, against the striking dark beauty of the young woman in the next cell. "I guess it would be hard to determine if they were specifically your ancestors in that grave?"

"What's that supposed to mean?"

She reminded him of a spiny lobster he'd once tried to tag. He recalled how fiercely it had wielded its formidable defenses.

"Nothing," he replied. He dropped the bars and wandered back into his cell. He stood with hands in his pockets for a moment, feeling at odds with himself. He sat on the bench that ran across the back wall, lost in his own thoughts.

Her voice cut through the twilight.

"Who *are* you, anyway?"

"David Tanaki," he said absently, then thinking aloud, "Why would they give such special treatment to the bones?"

"That's where the spirit lived."

He turned. "What about you? What do you call yourself?"

"Melanie Kersey. With white people, anyway."

"Do you think I'm white?"

"I'm not sure."

"Tell you the truth, I'm not either. I'm not even sure what it all means. But you have another name? An Indian one?"

She scuffed her boots across the floor. "Yeah, but it never seemed to fit. Seemed too prissy. Since I've been in the movement I'm using it more. My grandfather says the morning I was born there was a quarter moon rising . . . but what's that got to do with anything? Call me Melanie."

Tanaki would have liked to know more, but she was in the process of reclining on the bench, her face to the wall. Realizing his own fatigue, he leaned back, allowing his body to experience the let-down that was bound to follow the adrenal rush of the afternoon. He stretched out with his arms under his head; his thoughts splintered into a hazy collage of the day's confusion. He was asleep in moments.

He awoke to the sound of Valerie's voice heard through a fog of half-consciousness. He struggled to focus on her blurred image, which was further complicated by the pattern of bars between them. She wore a powder-blue suit. Her hair was in a pony tail. She looked real sweet, standing there smiling, saying his name. "David . . . time to wake up."

He got up and walked over to the bars. "I guess you're going to want to know how I got into this." He tried to chuckle, but it sounded like the constricted venting of air out of a balloon.

"I'll have to—if I'm going to get you out of here."

He walked back to the bench while the deputy opened the cell door. Valerie entered and sat down. He was explaining the events of the day in halting, jagged phrases when the deputy reappeared. He spoke as he opened the door.

"Good news. You're free."

He didn't look at Tanaki. Instead, his eyes moved from the lock to the floor, then to Melanie Kersey, who'd roused herself at the sound of the keys jangling in the lock. He smiled at her. She returned the gesture with a deliberate grimace.

Tanaki looked at Valerie. It seemed too sudden. She hadn't done her lawyerly stuff yet. Or had she worked a deal before coming to the jail? She turned to the deputy.

"You're releasing him?"

"That's right."

"What about the charges?"

"Been dropped."

Tanaki felt almost cheated. It seemed so anticlimactic. He was beginning to protest when Valerie drowned him out.

"Thank you very much, Officer," she said as she rose. "If you'll just give my client a moment to collect his things."

She stepped toward the door, waiting for Tanaki.

"Wait," he said, looking at the deputy. "What about her?" He nodded toward the next cell.

"What about her?"

"Isn't she getting out?"

Valerie stared hard at Tanaki, trying to silence him while maintaining a pleasant smile for the benefit of the deputy.

"Didn't receive no instructions about the girl."

Tanaki beckoned Valerie to the back of the cell. "Look, I got her into this mess. I think we ought to try to get her out of it."

"David," she whispered, "they don't take to outsiders coming down here and telling them how to take care of their business. I think you'd better get out of here while you can. I'll see what I can do for her. I just need a couple of days."

She looked at Melanie, who affected a bored, detached air.

With Tanaki at a loss for words, Valerie took him by the arm and directed him through the cell door. He wanted to offer Melanie some kind of assurance, but the situation seemed to call for an immediate exit. The deputy escorted him and Valerie down the hallway. When they reached the lobby Valerie turned and addressed the officer. "I'm with the university's legal defense project. Know that your staff will be held fully accountable for that woman's safety." She calmly turned and she and Tanaki descended the steps of the jailhouse. Her sports car was sitting at the curb with the top down. "I thought you said they don't like people coming down here—" he began. "I just couldn't help it," she said tersely as she pulled keys from her purse. Tanaki stopped for a moment and drew in the deliciously cooling air. She opened his door and pressed it closed after he was ensconced in the bucket seat. As they coursed over the asphalt rivers of Bristol County she thought out loud.

"Why would they have dropped the charges? That's really

weird. I can't imagine it's simply because you're affiliated with the research center." She reached down and turned off the radio, cogitation covering her face like a cloud. "Tell me more about the construction site."

Tanaki explained the equipment, the upturned earth, the hard hats.

"This just doesn't add up," she said. "That entire area is off-limits to new construction." She pulled at her hair tie and shook out her hair. Her face lightened. "I don't know, maybe someone got some kind of exception. It's late. I'll look into it tomorrow."

They cruised past dark woods interspersed with wayside settlements.

"Why don't we find a room in one of these little motels?" Tanaki asked, reaching over the console, laying his hand in her lap.

"Better not," she said, keeping her hands on the wheel. "I've got classes in the morning."

He delicately drew back his hand.

"David," she said after an awkward silence, "I like you in many ways. We have some important things in common. But I've been dwelling on our trip to the beach. I can appreciate your caring about those birds, but when I spend that kind of time with a man, I need a little more attention to be paid."

He couldn't manage to respond.

"I don't want to make a big deal about it," she said. "I'm just struggling with some boundary issues. Why don't we see if we can be friends for now."

"Sure, that's fine," he said, but he knew a brush-off when he heard one. He turned and watched the passing shadows as they sped toward Cambridge.

# 15

# *Be the bird*

It had started with the Bluebird soon after the waxwing invasion.

It was then she began using the phrase "Be the bird."

Of course Tanaki had also been affected by the events of that day. His loss of identity, the look in the Bluebird's eyes, the strange rapture of their lovemaking. In fact, he'd wandered around for days suffering from a sort of temporary amnesia, oblivious to his day-to-day obligations, uncertain who he was. He even avoided the Bluebird, in spite of several telephone messages. He felt he had to be alone. It had been too powerful. He couldn't digest it and he was worried.

Finally the Bluebird sent a telegram. "Must see you. Everything strange. A little scary. Quit hiding. Blue—."

They met in Bruges over the weekend. In spite of his trepidation, when he saw her coming across the courtyard in front of the hotel something melted away, all sense of danger dispelled, any urge to fight for his individuality gone, nothing left but the need to hold her, to be with her. They walked the cobbled streets of the town, skirting the canals and standing on small arching bridges watching the swans.

The call from Moeller came a couple months later. At the sound of his greeting Tanaki conjured a vivid image of his immaculately groomed, Old World polish.

"I don't want to worry you," he began, "but I want to talk to you about Ani."

"Ani?"

"I hope you won't find this—how shall I say—presumptuous is the word, I believe?"

The question was a rhetorical stall—Moeller's English was impeccable.

"No, please go on."

"Thank you, David. I knew I could count on you." He coughed. "As I said, it's about Ani."

"Right."

"It seems you and she have become, how shall I put it, quite close?"

Another rhetorical question. He and the Bluebird, while not brazenly thrusting their affair into the faces of their colleagues, had made no particular attempt to hide it. In fact, Tanaki was convinced that Moeller and Pannenburg had secretly abetted their romance in mysterious ways. Joint projects suddenly materialized, requiring close collaboration, and the Bluebird said she hadn't intrigued in arranging them. Tanaki knew he hadn't—not that he wouldn't have liked to: he simply hadn't been clever enough to pull it off. In the occasional paranoid moment he even wondered whether their older colleagues—their mentors, in fact—hadn't somehow orchestrated the affair as part of a private research agenda. Or on a bet. The two of them loved that sort of thing anyway. He could picture the many occasions, sitting in some cafe, when they'd place large wagers on when the first wheatear would appear, or who would receive some academic appointment. And they both loved discussing sex in all its permutations. Moeller particularly loved placing human lovemaking in the broader context of mammalian mating, and reveled in coming up with witty comparisons between human behaviors and those of other animals. It more amused than both-ered Tanaki to think that, even prior to his meeting the Bluebird, these two graying observers of life may have placed a healthy wager on how long it would take them to hop in the sack. He just hoped he hadn't disappointed them. And he wondered: did they have money riding on when the relationship would end?

"Go on . . ." he said warily.

"It's just that I've been noticing that Ani has been acting a little, shall I say, *unusual* lately." Distress was clawing its way through Moeller's veneer of calm control.

Tanaki remained guarded. "In what way?"

"Yes, that's just it. It's hard to describe." There was a nervous hitch in his voice.

"Go ahead and tell me what's on your mind, Dietrich. I can see you're concerned."

"Thank you, David. I knew . . . It's the cage, you see, the cage . . ."

"Which cage?"

"*Zugenruhe* . . . it's the *Zugenruhe* . . ."

"What? The cage you use for *Zugenruhe* experiments?"

"Yes, that's it. Thank you. I knew I could . . ."

"Dietrich?"

"Yes?"

"What about the *Zugenruhe* cage?"

"She's in it."

"Who? You mean the Blue—I mean, Ani, she's in the *Zugen-ruhe* cage?"

"Yes, exactly. That's it."

"What's she doing? Cleaning it?"

"No, David."

"Dietrich, please, tell me. What's she doing?"

"Please, hold the line a moment."

Tanaki heard the receiver being set down. Then he heard an extension picked up.

"Are you still there? Listen."

Now Moeller must have taken the phone from his ear, because in response to his questions Tanaki heard nothing but the hollow echo of Moeller's cavernous lab, built with high ceilings like an aviary, a hollowness he'd come to associate with phone calls from the Bluebird. For a moment he heard nothing else, then he slowly became aware of a rattling of metal. Then a loud "chirp," and another. There was something wildly plaintive about the call. But it was no bird Tanaki recognized. The chirping continued, changing rhythm, varying in volume. Moeller's voice came on the line.

"That's her."

"That's Ani?"

"Yes David. Please come quickly. I'm afraid something is terribly wrong."

Tanaki didn't bother to ask Pannenburg's permission to borrow the jeep. It wasn't clear what was going on at Moeller's lab, but the quavering quality of the great scientist's voice had shaken him. His mind raced as he sped toward Cologne, groping for an explanation for those bizarre chirps. He thought back over the last few months.

He'd managed to shake off the events associated with the waxwing invasion after the weekend in Bruges. He'd decided to classify the experience as an extremely interesting phenomenon, worthy perhaps of further thought when he had more time and leisure, but for the time being filed away in a nice, secure box in his mind. He was working with a group of Swedish biologists with whom he was reprising Perdecci's classic experiment, but with more sophisticated controls. He considered the study paramount to his career, and felt he couldn't let anything get in the way of its successful completion. He was following the only tried and true method he knew. He had an agenda, and he was sticking with it.

The Bluebird had reacted differently.

Over the course of the summer she'd lost interest in scientific studies in which only weeks before she was passionately involved. She took a wry interest in Tanaki's enthusiasm for the experiments he was organizing with the Swedes. After he described, in great detail, the lengthy preparations that would soon be underway, all the ingenious controls he and his colleagues had devised, she looked at him as one might look at a child, leaning back on the day bed in his room, and said, "Why not simply be the bird?"

"I can understand—conceptually, that is—what you're getting at," he said, "but I really don't see how you expect me to put it into practice."

She smiled at him.

"Well?" He stood looking at her, his hand held out as if waiting to receive something tangible.

"Honestly, David, I'm not sure either." She made an exaggerated frown, mocking his seriousness.

When they loved each other, she urged him to find that place again where they'd been on the day of the waxwings. Holding him, she would coo softly into his ear, or make fevered fluttering sounds as she ran her fingertips along his back. He tried to ignore it, kissing her passionately, as if by main force he could obliterate an experience that threatened to turn his world into chaos. He felt a pull toward some vortex from which he was sure they would never return. He was prepared to resist to the death.

Then she began a series of unorthodox—to say the least— experiments. She attempted to live on the diet of a bird for an entire week. Nothing but worms, seeds and berries. Later, against his strident objections, she began having Tanaki take her out in the jeep and drop her at remote places with which she was unfamiliar. Then she'd attempt to find her way back to the station without looking at road signs or consulting a map, while he worried himself sick. Most of these outings ended with a tired phone call in the middle of the night, telling a relieved Tanaki she was in such-and-such a town, would he please pick her up. But on one occasion she arrived triumphantly at the station after two days, smiling and waving as she emerged over a dune.

As autumn approached Tanaki became increasingly involved in preparations for the experiments with the Swedes. He began losing patience with the Bluebird. He felt his reputation, perhaps his entire career, was riding on the study. The Bluebird's recent fascinations, and her rejection of the methods she and Tanaki once shared, left him alone in his preoccupations. One day he exploded.

"Damn it, Bird, I'm getting tired of hearing about this be the bird crap. Maybe it'd be better if you just kept it to yourself."

She was stunned. The era of gentle playmates was over. Tanaki tried to explain. "Listen. I'm really jammed up with this study. And frankly, I feel like you've gone over the deep end. The stuff you've been talking about is kookiness, not science."

"I'm glad you told me the way you feel."

He should have held her then. He knew that. But he didn't. Somehow it wasn't part of the logic of the situation. His study was supposed to start soon—had to start, you couldn't tell birds when to migrate—and he couldn't waste time with the Bluebird's moodiness. He'd deal with it later, when the study was completed. He picked up his pen and continued writing in his notebook while she collected her things. She touched him on the shoulder as she walked past and said goodbye so quietly he wasn't sure whether he heard or merely imagined it.

"I'll call you,' he said without looking up.

That was the last time they'd spoken. He allowed himself to wonder hopefully, as he approached Cologne, if the routine in the cage wasn't some kind of a joke. A little gag to break the icy silence that had reigned between them for two weeks. But that didn't seem to square with the frightened tone of Moeller's voice, or the unearthly quality of the chirping he'd heard over the phone.

# 16

# *Nanticokes*

The facts surrounding Tanaki's arrest and detention awakened no small amount of curiosity in Valerie. The day after securing his release, she spent the afternoon working in the university's law library, digging out information on land use on the lower Shore. She found no record of any exceptions to the moratorium on development. From Tanaki's description, the construction project was significant. It sounded like a good four or five acres had been cleared, with several earth-moving machines on the site.

Was some renegade builder operating in flagrant violation of the law?

Why were charges against Tanaki so suddenly dropped?

The next morning she made calls to various offices in the state bureaucracy but no one seemed to know anything about the matter—or wish to discuss it. She called Tanaki to confirm the location of the site. He reminded her that Melanie Kersey was still languishing in the county jail. She let him know she was already working on the matter.


The sun was at its zenith in a pale blue sky as she zoomed along the sticky asphalt of a deserted county road. A dragonfly hovered above the windshield for a split second before disappearing in the rush of wind that sculpted the body of the car.

She listened to the radio while scanning the side of the road for the landmarks by which Tanaki had described the construction site: a white frame house with a spotted dog on the porch and a large barn in need of paint in the back; a broken-down pickup of antique vintage on cinder blocks; a sharp curve in the road; a stretch of pine forest; then the site.

She made note of each of the landmarks as she passed them—the frame house—the spotted dog, running alongside the road, yapping at her wheels—the barn in back—the pickup— the stand of loblollies, branches and needles waving in the mild breeze—and then—nothing! She pulled off the road and stared at the clearing that followed the stand of pines. She turned off the radio. Sure, there was a clearing. That much checked out. But there was no sign of construction equipment, nor of any other human endeavor. What's more, the ground didn't appear to have been disturbed, and was in fact covered with grass.

She took a hard look at the directions Tanaki had given her over the phone, mentally counting off the turns she'd taken, enumerating the landmarks, right down to the frame house with the dog, the barn, the pickup, and the pine grove. She was certain she'd come to the place he'd described. She drove directly to the county records office, hesitating only long enough to note the street address of the frame house so she'd have some point of reference for the grassy plot.

Sitting at a battered table, surrounded by dusty files, she located the parcel's plat, determined the plat number, and searched the files for ownership. The parcel had recently changed hands. It was now owned by a corporation listed as Seabreeze, Inc.—aside from a popular line of cosmetics, the corporate moniker incited no reverberations. She'd have to stop in Annapolis on the way back to Baltimore and check the state's incorporation records. From the land records office she walked across the town square to the courthouse, then to the bail bondsman's office. She arrived at the jailhouse in late afternoon, presenting some papers to the deputy at the front desk.

"I'll have to clear this," he said.

"I understand," she replied. "Can I go back while you take care of it?"

"Don't see why not."

Melanie Kersey was sitting on the bench at the back of the cell, slouching against the wall. She didn't bother to straighten up when Valerie approached.

"Look who it is," she said, looking up through her dark shades, "I suppose you're here to straighten out boyfriend's mess."

"But Ms. Kersey, I'm here to help *you* . . ."

Melanie stood up, removing her shades as she slowly approached the bars. "I didn't ask for your help," she said, "just like I didn't ask for your boyfriend's help. If he hadn't played the hero asshole and almost gotten three county cops killed, I wouldn't be here." She turned and sighed, then resumed in a philosophical vein, as if reasoning with herself. "Of course I should have expected he'd get off, with his high priced lawyer."

"Now Ms. Kersey . . ." Valerie tried to protest, speaking at her back.

"And I should have known what I'd get," Melanie continued, ignoring Valerie. "The same bullshit we Indians have always got. The shaft." Having concluded, she stared out the window, hoping Valerie would go away.

Valerie let the silence sink in. She wasn't insensitive to Melanie's remarks. She was familiar with the history of First Americans on the Eastern Shore, and was aware that like First Americans all over the continent, they'd invariably gotten the short end of the stick in their dealings with technologically and numerically superior Euro-Americans. She too turned around, leaned against the bars, and ran through a brief history of the Nanticoke people in her mind, searching through that shrouded fog for some clue to the psyche of the young woman caged on the other side of the bars.

The original inhabitants of the Eastern Shore had accommodated the first English settlers, but relations between the two groups were soon marred by the colonists' sharp trade practices, the relentless encroachment of English settlements on traditional hunting grounds, and the marauding of the settlers' cattle through the Nanticokes' gardens of beans and maize. Though most of these occurrences were small fare, on several occasions the conflicts erupted into open warfare.

In the early eighteenth century, Maryland's British governor tried to establish harmony on the Shore by establishing a reservation along Chicawan Creek, a Nanticoke River tributary, where the Nanticokes could live unmolested by the newcomers. But he failed to protect their rights from his capital on the opposite side of the bay. So when they received an offer to join the Iroquois nation on the banks of the Susquehanna, most of them packed up and migrated northward. A few dozen diehards stayed behind, reluctant to leave the land where their ancestors' bones rested. But eventually these hardy souls were forced off the reserved lands by avaricious colonists. They settled to the east around Indian River, where having adopted the ways of the European settlers, they gained their subsistence from farming and fishing. They lived there inconspicuously until shortly before the Civil War, when the vicious dynamics of racism brought an unwelcome scrutiny to their community.

Lewis Sockum was a Nanticoke who lived at Indian River. A profitable general store and a number of shrewd land purchases had made him a rare success, and a target for the greed and envy of white neighbors. In the midst of the racial paranoia that followed John Brown's raid at Harper's Ferry he was accused of selling gunpowder to his son-in-law, who, the state averred, was a mulatto, and not allowed to possess firearms. The copper toned

Sockum countered that Isaac Harmon was in fact a Nanticoke Indian, like himself.

The state's key witness was a frail old woman named Lydia Clark, reputed to be the sole Nanticoke still conversant in the native tongue. Her testimony, given under duress of eviction by her prominent white landlord, began with an Irish widow named Chancey who, after the revolution, owned a plantation not far from Indian River. On hearing of a slave ship stranded on the bar, so the story went, Chancey hied herself to the waterfront in hopes of acquiring a field hand. To complete the faery tale, the handsome man she selected was a prince of one of the Congo tribes, and before the season turned she was big with their first child. A dozen more followed—so Lydia testified—and the mixed children of this illicit romance, shunned by the white community, took husbands and wives from among the Indian River Nanticokes. Lydia testified that not only Isaac Harmon, but Lewis Sockum and all the other Nanticokes living around Indian River, were the issue of these marriages, rendering them "colored" under the "one-drop-of-blood" theory enshrined in state law. The court accepted the story, ignoring Clark's simultaneous assertions that both Sockum and Harmon were Nanticoke Indians like herself. Sockum was fined twenty dollars for selling powder to his son-in-law. What was worse, he was likewise declared "colored" and deprived of the right to bear arms. Unwilling to bow to this novel oppression, he sold out and left the state in disgust.

If there was a bright side to the tale, the trial shook the Indian River community out of its complacency. For the first time, the Nanticokes organized to protect their rights. And Lewis Sockum became the first and greatest hero of the Indian River people: the demonstration that landed Melanie in jail, in fact, could be traced back to the activism inspired by his trial.

But she had no way of knowing, as she stared out the window

of her cell, that the impeccably dressed city woman on the other side of the bars knew more about the history of her people than most of her relations. Valerie had been teaching a seminar on the development of property rights in the state for years, and owed her job at the university to her dissertation for the LLB: "Trouble in the Garden: Planters and Nanticokes, 1631-1789."

"Ms. Kersey," Valerie began, turning into the bars, "I know you have every reason to be upset. The legacy of the sort of thing that happened to Lewis Sockum isn't altogether over. But if we work together, I think we can make some of today's battles come out a little better."

Melanie turned, looking at Valerie with a mixture of skepticism and amazement.

"I'm just beginning to investigate what went on at the burial grounds the other day," Valerie continued, "but it already smells bad."

"What'd you find out?" Melanie asked desperately.

"They've stopped digging, and covered up everything, like it never happened."

"What?" Melanie said, revolving on herself.

"I have a mind to stay on this thing until I figure it out," Valerie said. "And I'll be happy to help your group with the legal end of things."

"What'll it cost us?"

"Nothing."

"Are you serious?"

"Of course. We can work it through the university's legal defense project. But I'm going to need your help. So let's get out of here."

"There's no way I can come up with the bail money."

"I didn't have a chance to mention," Valerie said, digging her keys out of her purse. "The bail's taken care of."

Melanie stood dumbstruck for a moment, then said

energetically, "I'll pay you back." A film of tears had formed over her eyes.

The deputy was coming down the hallway. Melanie collected her things while he unlocked the door. She ignored him as she left the cell, addressing Valerie.

"I totally blew the passive resistance thing," she said, laughing through her tears.

"I'm sure it's not easy," Valerie said. "But you put yourself on the line for what you believe in. I admire that."

Melanie put an arm around Valerie's waist and touched her head briefly onto her shoulder as they strolled out of the cell block. "Do me one more favor, will you?"

"What's that?"

"Find your boyfriend something hipper to read than *Albion's Spawn in the Great Shellfish Bay*."

Valerie was about to protest that Tanaki wasn't her boyfriend, but instantly thought better of leaving the field open. "He's reading that?" she asked incredulously.

The two broke into girlish laughter as they left the jailhouse, the deputy looking on in dumb wonder.

## 17

# *Revolt*

As July melted quietly into August, Folker's regime had become so onerous not only to Tanaki, but to his colleagues on the Center's staff, that a clandestine meeting was organized to discuss the situation. Tanaki was notified by DeForrest, who casually approached his research cube one afternoon holding a piece of orange paper through the doorway as he whistled nonchalantly. Tanaki wheeled his chair over and took the flyer with a puzzled look. He unfolded it and read the large capital letters:

> FOR ALL OF YOU WHO ARE
> SICK AND TIRED
> OF THE INCESSANT
> AND UNNECESSARY
> MEDDLING WHERE HIS %#*@*
> DOES NOT BELONG
> OF OUR SO-CALLED
> "DIRECTOR"
> MEET FOR DISCUSSION—
> IN THE CANTEEN AT FOUR
> THIS AFTERNOON

Tanaki couldn't help but smile at the animus expressed in the announcement. In his effort to maintain a professional demeanor he'd failed to take stock of how angry Folker was making him.

He nodded affirmatively to DeForrest and turned to look out on the bay. Small whitecaps danced on the aquamarine surface. He recalled that Folker, accompanied by Cynthia, was in Annapolis for meetings, and felt a surprising thrill at the idea of holding a gripe session in their absence.

When he entered the canteen a couple minutes before four, many of his colleagues were already there. Several had been out and around the bay to judge from the sun on their faces, the splotches of mud on their clothes, and the fatigue in their postures. A few were leaning against the vending machines that lined one wall, others were seated at the half-dozen or so tables that occupied the better part of the room.

Tanaki recognized them all, though he didn't know any of them well. They'd chatted on the occasion of chance encounters in this room, in the supplies room, or around the docks. He'd seen them at staff meetings and consulted a few about their research. But he hadn't really socialized with any of them. He worked late so often, and most of them were married or otherwise occupied. Besides, on his rare evenings off, he found himself looking forward to dinner at the Yamaguchis.

At the far end of the room Beth Delantis sat at a table with a fan of paper in front of her. She wrote industriously, looking up from time to time to gauge attendance. Tanaki had passed a couple of profitable and pleasant hours one afternoon picking her brain on her specialty, planktonic life. She'd been at the Center for several years. She spent a lot of time peering through a microscope, when she wasn't out collecting specimens. Her face was browned by hours in the sun and salt air.

Shortly DeForrest came through the door. Beth noticed him, made eye contact, and raised her eyebrows in a questioning gesture. With a nod DeForrest indicated it was time to begin. He turned and closed the door, and Delantis spoke.

"I guess you all know why we're meeting here."

A chorus of "Oh yes's" and "Mmm-hmm's."

"I've taken some time to draw up a short list of our griev-ances. If it's okay with you, I'll start by reading it and getting your input."

Affirmative nods.

"Here it is. Number one: Unexplained and unprecedented interference with our research schedules."

More nods.

"Number two: Incessant requests to do public relations work."

Inarticulate grumblings.

"Number three: Failure to communicate policy to staff in a cogent fashion."

"You mean any fashion . . ." someone blurted from near the Coke machine.

"Number four: Bogus rationales for previously stated inter-ference."

Raised eyebrows.

Her voice grew quiet. "Number five: a growing sense of paranoia?"

She looked up, seeking the eyes of her colleagues. They looked at the floor or otherwise averted their eyes from her per-sistent gaze. Perhaps she was striking too close to the heart of the matter.

Tanaki sensed the discomfort in the room but didn't share it. To the contrary, he felt strangely energized. Having buckled under to Folker's meddling all spring and summer, trying not to be the damned nail sticking up, he experienced a sense of lib-eration in Beth's rebelliousness. When her eyes scanned to his he didn't waiver but returned her gaze, smiling calmly and nod-ding slowly, affirmatively. She didn't avert her eyes either, but returned his smile. Then, continuing to look at him, she said, "So what are we going to do about this?"

Tanaki felt the collective attention of his colleagues bearing down on him, led there by Beth's unabated gaze. He felt a sense of implosion, as if the weight of all those stares were compressing something inside him, forcing the essence of his being into a tighter and tighter bundle, until release was the only natural consequence. Suddenly all the expectation in the faces of his colleagues became irrelevant. He even ceased to notice Beth's continuing stare. He pushed back his chair and rose to speak.

"I don't know what everyone else is thinking," he heard himself say, "but I say we've got to make some kind of protest. I can tell you that Folker's meddling has played hell with my research already, and if I don't start getting down to the lower bay sometime soon I may as well write off the entire season."

His colleagues made small rustling noises.

"I mean, I've done research in a lot of settings, and I've never seen anything like this. Either this man is crazy, some kind of control freak, or there's something else going on."

"What do you mean, something else?" Beth asked.

"I'm not sure. But this whole experience with Folker has an aura of unreality about it. You ask for explanations, and you get some story about the Coast Guard, or the weather service. And we're not idiots, after all. We can see the weather's not bad. I'm starting to feel like we're being gas-lighted or something."

"Do you have any suggestions?"

"For starters, somebody's got to talk to him, confront him with all this, and not take any bull for an answer."

Beth looked around the room. "Any volunteers?" People shifted in their chairs, the standing ones moved their weight from one foot to the other.

DeForrest spoke up. "Why don't you speak to him, Dave? You seem to have a pretty good handle on the situation."

Tanaki looked around the room. His colleagues looked at him as though they were in a hopelessly besieged town and he was about to be sent through enemy lines for help. Moved by their haplessness, but with a sense that he was over-extending himself, he agreed to present the staff's grievances to Folker. He also agreed to report his findings at another meeting to be arranged as circumstances might permit.

There was no question of seeing Folker immediately; he'd be at the conference in the capital for several days. Tanaki was grateful for this, because after the meeting broke up and everyone stood chatting over cokes and chips, he knew he'd done it again, gotten himself involved in something beyond his main agenda: migration research. In his mind, he ticked off the events like the beads on a rosary: the impassioned speech in Baltimore the day he met Valerie; the episode at the beach with the gulls and the trash; and most recently, his run-in with the law over Melanie Kersey and her protester friends. He felt a vague sense of fear, like being at sea with someone else at the helm, someone whose face you may never see, whose voice you may never hear, whom you are certain you know intimately. He'd once known what he was about. He knew there was a big world outside his quiet investigation, but he'd always been sure it was nothing he wanted to get mixed up in. He thought about Melanie. She was still sitting in the county jail as far as he knew. And what about Haskel, a prisoner in his own house, beleaguered at every step, his lawn covered with geese guano, his wife perennially visiting friends and relatives. Then there was the Bluebird—and the mere thought of her came like a stab at his heart. Look what her originality had gotten her. There was a line it seemed you couldn't cross without risking personal difficulty, inconvenience, or in the worst possible case, annihilation. His father wasn't without reason, he thought. There was a certain comfort in being down there with all the other nails. Now he'd gone and done it again, thrust himself right into hammer range. As the Honda coasted down Talbot Street he forcibly put the meeting with Folker out of his mind. He'd cross that bridge when he came to it.

When he entered his apartment he noticed the red light blinking in the twilight. He strode directly to the answering machine and pressed play. After a couple seconds of static Valerie's voice came over the speaker, pinched and far away.

"David—Valerie. I've been looking into that construction site. Nothing very definitive yet, but things are looking strange. I'll keep you posted. And oh—I took care of your girlfriend down in Bristol. She really loves you to death, the operative word being death . . . (laughter) . . . I'll talk to you soon."

Tanaki sat down and watched the dark forms of magnolia branches moving languidly in the breeze. Valerie's crack about Melanie reverberated in his ears. He thought they'd gotten onto a pretty friendly basis before he left the jail. "I guess after being locked up a couple more days . . ." he thought. He was overcome by an urge to apologize for the trouble he'd caused, but settling back in his over-stuffed chair he wondered why he should feel such concern for someone he'd hardly gotten to know. She was attractive, but probably too young for him. And there wasn't much common ground there. She seemed the epitome of the local girl, and he was anything but a local boy. All the more reason he couldn't understand why the idea of seeking her out, making things up to her, seemed to come to the foreground of his consciousness, temporarily crowding out every other concern, even his research, even the meeting with Folker. But perhaps that explained it, he thought. Couldn't the entire thing be a trick his mind was playing, relieving itself of anxieties over real issues in his life by conveniently substituting this tangential concern, then focusing his attention there?

It was nine o'clock. He switched on the lamp and picked up a book he'd been reading, *Albion's Spawn or Caliban's Scourge?: New Reflections on English Colonization in the Chesapeake.*

# 18

# *Joe Pasquath*

He awoke in the morning with one thought on his mind: find Melanie Kersey. He lay in bed looking at the ceiling. "If this is a trick my mind is playing on me, it's a damned persistent one," he said out loud. He tried closing his eyes, hoping he'd fall into some dream and wake up thinking about getting to work, but it wasn't any good. He couldn't shake the idea of Melanie. He had a feeling that if he could talk to her, explain himself, everything would turn out fine—his research, the difficulties with Folker, even his eel-tracking study. Of course there was nothing logical in that expectation. But it was as real as the sunlight falling on the bedroom floor, as the birds singing out back.

And of course there were practical difficulties to be considered. He had no idea where he might find Melanie. He didn't know where she lived—not even remotely. He could ask Valerie, but then again . . .

In the shower he devised a strategy that wasn't particularly clever but which struck him as such, so unused was he to intrigue. He decided to call Valerie and tell her a white lie, something about having wound up with one of Melanie's belongings. When he returned to his bedroom, wrapped in a towel, he looked at the clock beside the bed. It was seven o'clock. He figured Valerie would still be at home. He searched through the scraps of paper scattered on the nightstand. He'd only called a couple of times and didn't know the number by heart.

She sounded groggy when she answered. He told her he'd found a piece of what looked like Native American jewelry stuck in the laces of the tennis shoes he was wearing the day of his arrest. "I guess it must have fallen while we were on the dozer," he said.

Valerie yawned.

"It looks like an earring," he was inventing as he went along, "the hook part somehow got caught in the laces."

"It's funny you didn't notice."

"I know. I guess it's the color. It kind of blends in. Anyway, I thought I'd get the address so I could drop it in the mail."

"It's probably just inexpensive costume jewelry. I don't think you need to worry about it." Her voice was warm, Tanaki's room oddly barren.

"But it looks like it could be valuable. Besides, I feel like I've given the kid enough grief."

"Alright. Hold on a minute."

She put down the phone. He pictured her walking around the room in her nightgown, drowsy and fuzzy, and felt lousy lying to her. She came back on the line.

"David?"

"Yeah, I'm here."

"You're not interested in this girl, are you?"

He tried to sound jocular. "Valerie, come on, I just want to return the jewelry."

"Good," she replied laughing, "because she really thinks you're strange."

The address was in Salisbury, one of the larger Eastern Shore towns, about a half-hour down the highway toward the beach. Tanaki decided to go directly there after getting dressed and having breakfast. He didn't call first, figuring she might blow him off. He knew if he showed up in person he'd be more likely to get a hearing.

It was going on ten when the Honda pulled up in front of the squat, brick buildings that sat at the end of a road that went nowhere, just after a railroad crossing. There was no one out and about. Everything was quiet except for the sound of birds in the battered locust trees that stood haphazardly along the dusty street. The sun was bright but the heat still at a manageable level when he stepped out of the car. He crossed the street, entered the building, and climbed to the second floor. A tousled young woman in a baggy sweatshirt answered the door and looked at him through bleary eyes, straining to make out his features in the dark stairwell.

"Hi, I'm looking for Melanie."

"Who are you?" she asked forthrightly.

"I'm a friend of hers."

"Are you part of the Nanticoke Association?"

He told his second lie of the day.

"She's at her grandfather's . . ."


The grandfather lived in a remote area near Chicawan Creek, that tributary of the Nanticoke River around which the ill-fated reservation had been established in colonial days. Tanaki took several blacktop roads past farmsteads and chicken coops before turning onto a dusty, rutted road that ran through pines and hardwoods. As he approached the creek the nature of the forest changed, with a greater admixture of ash and hackberry, and the pungently sweet odor of damp soil filled the air. Where the road ended an old blue compact was parked against the brush. He stepped out of the Honda and heard the soft rippling of water. There was a footpath through the woods. A wooden marker in the shape of an arrow, covered with cracked white paint, was affixed to a tree at its head.

The path slowly converged toward the rippling sound as he walked over the leaf mould that covered the ground, taking in the profusion of insect and bird calls that filled the woods. After a hundred yards glimpses of a crude dwelling appeared through the trees. He felt uneasy approaching unannounced, an intruder in these quiet woods, disturbing Melanie's visit to her grandfather. But whatever had propelled him this far—to call Valerie, to take the morning off from his research, to lie shamelessly twice in one day—propelled him onward through the trees.

He needn't have worried about arriving unannounced. As he came around a bend, which placed him on a line of sight with the shack he'd seen through the forest, a chorus of dog yelps shattered the silence of the woods. Three or four mongrels were mobilizing around the end of the path, furiously barking at the stranger who now leaned against a tree with one hand. Within moments Melanie appeared behind them, peering through the mottled light of the woods. Tanaki stepped into the middle of the path and waved one arm in a broad gesture, trying to look casual, as if to say, I was just driving by, thought I'd stop to say hello.

She strode toward him, yelping dogs preceding her steps. When she was ten feet away she asked over the snarling animals, "What are you doing here?"

He groped for words, indicating the hounds with a searching gesture of one arm. He finally managed to get out "Could we talk somewhere?"

She turned and walked toward the shack as she said over one shoulder, "Come on."

The dogs must have picked up a cue from Melanie, because they desisted in their persecutions. By the time they all reached the shack, in fact, he and the hounds had acquainted themselves in the most friendly fashion. When Melanie's grandfather emerged from the low shelter into the clearing which surrounded it, a laughing Tanaki was at the center of a whirl of leaping, yelping mutts.

"You're just like one of the animals," the old man said.

Tanaki was certain he was going to lay into him. He was about to protest that his intentions toward Melanie were on the up-and-up when the old man continued.

" . . . that's beautiful," he said, shaking his head and chuckling to himself as he laid out the dogs' food.

Tanaki felt Melanie wince at her grandfather's kind remark. "This is the guy who got me locked up a couple weeks ago," she said.

Her grandfather looked up at Tanaki from the dogs' dishes. "You might of done her a big favor."

"I don't know about that," a nonplussed Tanaki replied, feeling another wince from Melanie. The old man continued.

"Once you been caged, you really know what it's worth to be free."

His remark created a void. Tanaki looked around and noticed that the old man's shack sat only a few yards from the creek. It was a low structure of board which, had it ever been painted, showed no lingering signs of the operation. It had the appearance of being built in stages, with no overall unity of design between subsequent additions. Whatever integrity it possessed was on account of the tatterdemalion appearance of the whole. There were a few chickens pecking in the dirt and a wire cage in the back. A canoe lay in a patch of weeds near the creek.

The old man approached Tanaki and held out his hand. "I'm Joe Pasquath."

He was short, with a thin and wiry frame. His gray hair straggled over his ears and overlapped his collar in the back. His sunken cheeks, bony jaw, and knobby chin were covered with a prickly white stubble. He wore a pair of baggy old jeans and a loose fitting flannel shirt, in spite of the heat.

Tanaki introduced himself. Joe invited him in and asked Melanie to make some coffee. She preceded them over the threshold and disappeared into the relative darkness of the shack. Joe offered Tanaki a seat in the cabin's main room, and soon had him detailing his work at the Center, listening intently as Tanaki outlined all of his elaborate plans and procedures. Melanie stood in an adjoining alcove brewing coffee. After Tanaki enthusiastically described the eel experiment, Joe asked him to wait. He scrambled up, went through a doorway that came off the room at an odd angle, and returned with a cylindrically shaped piece of basketry about three feet long. He held it in front of his chest with a hand on either end.

"Ever seen one of these?" he asked, proffering the object for examination.

Tanaki revolved the cylinder in his lap and scrutinized both ends.

"Looks like some kind of trap," he said, glancing at Melanie for reasons he couldn't explain. She was pouring coffee from a steel kettle she'd just removed from a kerosene burner.

Joe nodded his head and smiled. "You can have it."

Tanaki wasn't sure what he'd do with it. After all, he wasn't much of a collector. He began to protest, "No, I couldn't."

"Go ahead. You can catch your eel in it."

Tanaki didn't want to hurt the old man's feelings, tell him the Center had far more sophisticated devices for trapping eels. He was about to thank him for the gift when Joe continued, "I know you got plenty of fancy devices for capturing animals at the research station, but none of 'em have the kind of magic this thing's got."

Melanie brought over coffee. "Grandpa," she said, sitting the cups on a table, "I doubt this guy's into that kind of stuff.

He's the scientific type." She shot Tanaki a glance as she walked back to the alcove.

He was about to protest, not out of any real disagreement, but because he didn't want to seem disrespectful of the old man. Joe pre-empted his response.

"Don't worry, I know about scientists. They believe in their own kind of magic. Only it doesn't always work." He laughed gently, as if to make certain Tanaki not read any bitterness into his observation. Tanaki smiled gamely, willing to take a little teasing.

"The real reason I came," he said, "was to apologize for having stuck my nose, obviously unsuccessfully, into Melanie's business last week."

She was tidying up the kitchen counter. "What's the point?" she asked. "It's over and done with."

"I guess I'm not sure," Tanaki responded earnestly.

Joe shifted his gaze from Melanie to Tanaki as each spoke, observing every nuance of their exchange unabashedly, almost scientifically. Tanaki continued with evident difficulty. "I don't know what's been getting into me lately. I end up doing something impulsively, without thinking ahead."

"What's wrong with that?" Joe interjected.

Melanie laughed. She came back into the room and stood over the men with hands on her hips. "It's some kind of control freak thing, I think, Grampa."

"What's wrong with that?" Joe repeated.

Melanie didn't respond.

Tanaki spoke. "I guess Melanie has a point."

She answered his gesture with a guarded smile.

"Maybe it's part of my work," Tanaki said, "or my work's part of me, I don't know. Control is largely what science is all about, trying to gain some control over the universe."

"But the more science we get, the more things seem to be

going haywire," Joe mused to no one in particular.

Melanie sat down with the men, then Joe resumed.

"Sure, scientists do a lot of amazing things—jet planes, satellites, all that. Some of you guys are even trying to save the bay. That's pretty powerful. But still everything seems to be going downhill." He fixed his eyes on the floor for a moment, then raised them, suddenly inspired. "Maybe it's because everybody's sitting around staring at TV, they don't notice what's going on. No matter how hard you try and save the bay, as long as people are staring at that box, you'll never win. They can't feel the bay through the box. They can't feel the earth."

Tanaki was getting uncomfortable. But before he could indulge the sensation, Joe stood up and patted him on the shoulder.

"You're a nice boy," he said. "You'd be good for Morning Moon."

Tanaki was so embarrassed he hardly registered Melanie's Indian name. Morning Moon, for her part, maintained a steady cool as she said sardonically, "Grampa, I think you're losing it."

As he drove back to Cambridge Tanaki tried to focus on the projects waiting for him at the lab. He and Reynolds had tests to run on the radio transmitters, and there were those trips to the lower bay, if he could find some way around Folker's interference.

But his mind kept drifting back to Joe Pasquath handing him that eel trap. That image, full-blown and fulgent, reappeared at interstices in his thoughts like the line of an ephemeral fugue. It pulled at him until he finally gave in to it, letting the memory of the transaction completely occupy his mind until it began to alternate with another, similar image. As in the first one, he was receiving an object from an old man. Only he was a teenager, and the old man wasn't Melanie's grandfather—he was his own.

The two of them were on a fishing pier. His grandfather was

handing him a bucket full of mullet.

Tanaki had gone to California to spend a couple of weeks of his fourteenth summer with his grandparents. He hadn't seen much of them growing up, and his parents feared that if he didn't visit soon he might never have the chance. They were getting on in years and neither of them was in the best of health.

He could picture his grandfather perfectly. Short and stocky, close-cropped white hair, mottled skin weathered by years working in the California sun, first on his farm, and then, after the war, doing landscaping work. He took Tanaki fishing several times during that summer's visit—what emerged from the depths of Tanaki's memory about this day was a conversation about Tanaki's father. He'd never really thought about the fact that his father had once been young himself. His father had never said much about his youth, and it had never occurred to Tanaki to ask.

He'd always seen his father, first and foremost, as a rule-maker, the source of all the strictures he tried so hard to abide in his yet callow life. The prophet of the nail that sticks up. A guy who'd figured out the system and went steadily about his life as an industrial engineer. There were enigmas, certainly, the odd moment when the guard came down and he was revealed in a more vulnerable light—like the night he had to be rushed to the hospital with an inflamed prostate, when he sat on the bed wrapped in wet towels that Tanaki's mother constantly replaced to bring down the fever—but these episodes were few and far between, and did little to challenge Tanaki's view of the family patriarch as a guy who had things under control.

The kind of male camaraderie that emerged on fishing trips brought him close to his father's most elemental being, but didn't tell him much about his private thoughts or experiences. So when his grandfather began to reminisce about the days before his father was his father, but was still merely Ken Tanaki, he listened with rapt attention, knowing he was receiving a precious gift, one that would probably never be offered again. It started with fish.

"You know your Dad always loved fishing."

"Me too."

His grandfather cast his line over the railing of the pier.

"You know, now that I think about it, being so far away from water probably didn't make the camp any easier for him."

"Camp?" His parents had never made any but the most elliptical allusions to their experiences during the war.

"Your folks never told you about the internment camp?"

"There was something about it in social studies, but when I brought it up with Mom and Dad they said it was over and done with and I should forget about it."

"I can understand your Dad not wanting to talk about it," the old man said, tugging tentatively on the rod. He reeled in his line and recast. "Of course we all hated it. But he got more worked up about it."

"Really?" Tanaki remarked. His father seemed too collected to have ever been worked up about anything.

"Not that I didn't know how he felt. It wasn't easy for your grandma and me selling the farm for pennies to the dollar. Folks coming round offering next to nothing for what we'd worked all our lives for, when they knew we only had a week to pack up and leave. Course they were getting what they'd wanted all along—to get rid of us Japs."

Tanaki suddenly stiffened. His grandfather freed one hand and squeezed him hard over the top of the shoulder, laughing through clenched teeth at his erstwhile neighbors' absurdities.

"What about Dad and that camp?" Tanaki asked, impatient to hear more about his father.

"It was out in the Arizona desert, and the sun beat down on you like a broiler. He couldn't get over the fact they made us Japanese live in camps during the war. It was more of a shock for some of the younger ones than for us older folks. We'd gone through the alien land law and the exclusion acts, and just more plain meanness. I don't know, maybe we still had more of the old *gaman* spirit in us."

"What's that?"

"It means sticking it out no matter what. Even with everything working against you." He tugged decidedly on his reel and grew more animated. "Just stick to the job and ignore it. No matter what the obstacles, just keep trying."

"It bugs me when I hear things like 'slant-eyes,'" Tanaki confided.

"It was worse in your Dad's day. Some of the rotten ones at school would call him Chink to his face, and when farms went up for sale, people put up signs saying Japs Stay Out. But your grandma and I told him to ignore it and concentrate on his studies. He was an American citizen—not a foreigner like us. I'd tell him it was a free country, and if he could prove he was good as anybody else they'd have to let him succeed."

He crouched down and cut some bait, then stood up and cast his line again.

"The real trouble started at the camp high school when he wouldn't sing that song with everyone. What's it called, 'Tis of thee' or something like that? 'My country,' that's the part he didn't like. Said if it was his country why was he locked up in some stinkin' cage. Your grandma and I had to go in and talk to the principal. We were worried sick about him. Sure he was ruining his chances. I tried to talk to him. I told him the nail that sticks up gets hammered down, but he wouldn't listen. He said, real excited, You told me to concentrate on my studies and I'd succeed. The only thing my blessed concentration got me was a concentration camp! I got so mad I did something I'd never done before. I hit him right across the face, hard as I could."

He stopped speaking and looked down, his mouth tightening

as if he were trying to swallow and couldn't. There was nothing but the sound of waves roiling below the pier, punctuated by seabirds' cries.

"After that he started staying away from home a lot. Hanging out with these boys who wanted to fight the system. Not cooperate with the authorities.

"Then they came around to recruit boys for the war. When this sergeant came by our place he got up in the guy's face and said—I'll always remember how he said it: What do you take us for? A bunch of idiots? You classify me enemy alien and lock me up like a wild animal, then expect me to volunteer for some suicide squad so I can get my butt shot off for your so-called democracy. That's going some for sheer nerve!"

The old man chuckled and spit over the pier's railing, seeming to relish the memory of his son's gutsiness. Tanaki, for his part, was mesmerized by this new image of his father, now firmly ensconced in corporate America, taking on the system. He urged his grandfather to go on.

"I was so mad I could hardly see straight. I was sure they'd get him after that—maybe take it out on the rest of the family too. But I couldn't talk to your Dad. He quit listening to me after that time I hit him. You know about your Uncle Frank?"

"He died in the war."

"That's right. After your Dad dressed that sergeant down everything was real quiet in our section of the barracks. I was still mad as hell. Your Dad—when he was home—wasn't talking to anybody. Your grandma paced around stewin' all day, worrying about me and your Dad fighting, and about what the authorities might do if they found out what he was up to with his new friends. She tried to make peace between us but I wouldn't give an inch and neither would your Dad. Frank couldn't stand seeing everybody upset. He was a sweet kid. Easy-going. And man was he fast—number one in track."

He looked out over the Pacific.

"I think the tension finally got to him. He went over to the recruitment office and enlisted. Figured if he signed on they'd let us alone. Your grandma was beside herself. When your Dad found out he tried to talk him out of it—said he'd go in his place—but it was too late, the army had him."

"What happened then?" Tanaki asked in a voice filled with awe and dread.

The old man began slowly, precisely, "Your Dad was right about those suicide squads. Frank was in the 442nd, all Japanese. They put those guys up against the toughest Nazi troops in Italy. They got chewed up real bad."

Tanaki could hear the old man's throat tightening. After peering into the water a moment he abruptly raised his eyes to the blank sky.

"But they did us proud—the most decorated unit in the whole damned war." He loudly cleared his throat. "When your Dad heard about Frank gettin' killed he wanted to kill some Germans real bad. He went down to the recruitment office and tried to enlist, but they had him figured for a troublemaker and wouldn't take him."

Tanaki exhaled loudly, "I never knew a thing about this."

"Funny some of the things parents don't think their kids oughta know," the old man said, glancing at his grandson. "I guess it's like when your Dad was growing up, I tried to make light of the troubles we had. Didn't want to spoil his view of his country. Maybe if I'd been more realistic the camp wouldn't have been such a shock."

They fished in silence until Tanaki's grandfather began speaking out of the blue.

"I remember one time after Frank died. I was out at the edge of the camp looking at the desert through the barbed wire. Sometimes I'd go there and just stand where it was quiet and let my mind wander. There was something about looking across all that land . . . reminded me there was more world out there. It was getting near evening and the light was kind of funny, the time of day when your eyes play tricks on you, especially in the desert.

"I was standing there not thinking about anything in particular, and I saw something coming toward me, real small in the distance. As it got closer I could tell it was a person walking toward me. I just stared. I couldn't figure who'd be out there because there was nothing but desert for miles around. But when they got closer it seemed they were wearing fatigues, so I begin to figure it was part of the camp guard. Then the guy starts running. Straight at me, with a big smile on his face. And then I recognize who it is—but it can't be. It's Frank, running toward me, holding his arms out like he's gonna give me a big hug. Soon as I realize it was him he up and disappeared on me.

"It was just a mirage but I cried like a damn baby."


Tanaki was half-way across the Choptank bridge before realizing he'd passed Cambridge. As he turned at a break in the median, he could see his grandfather standing at a barbed wire fence in the loneliness of the Arizona desert. He thought about Joe Pasquath's remark—"once you been caged, you really know what it's worth to be free."

When he got home he found a note from the Yamaguchis taped to his doorjamb. It was an invitation to "Sea Festival and Dinner" for the coming weekend. Wondering what "sea festival" might be, he wrote a short response on the same piece of notepaper, light blue with pastel flowers around the border, walked up the creaking stairs to the third floor, and taped it to the sisters' door using the original piece of scotch tape.

# 19

# Sea Festival

Saturday morning he walked to Yamaguchi Enterprises. The building was festooned with bunting, and a couple dozen modern fishing boats crowded around the docks, bright pennants flying from their spars and bridges. He walked through the front office and into the large, cavernous processing area behind. Setsuko was a good hundred feet away, giving instructions to a crowd of fifty or more men. They shook their heads in acknowledgement or just calmly listened. Tanaki remembered Margaret Brent handling the mutinous soldiers after Ingels' Rebellion.

Not wanting to get in the way of company business, he stayed near the door to the front office, quietly observing. One of the company's vessels bobbed gently at an indoor slip, decorated with banners and pennants like the ones in the harbor. Nariko emerged from around a corner and greeted him. She seemed in a good mood; there was a sort of glow he'd never noticed before.

She took him by the arm and led him to where Setsuko and her employees were moving toward the Ebisu shrine on the opposite wall. Nariko and Tanaki stopped short of the melee of movement that engulfed the god's abode. With Setsuko directing every move, the men split into four groups, each laying hold to one of the carrying posts, like those of a palanquin, that extended from each corner of the ornate structure. On Setsuko's three-count they crouched to maneuver the poles onto their shoulders and heaved the god into the air. Ebisu, though sorely bobbled, remained undisturbed, smiling in his maniacally gleeful way throughout the operation.

The deity was maneuvered to the boat in the interior dock, and with much grunting and groaning, much sidestepping and twisting and turning, was placed in a prominent position on the bow, face forward. The Yamaguchi crews secured the shrine with boat lines, then dispersed to take up positions on the vessels Tanaki had seen in the harbor—the entire strength of Yamaguchi Enterprises' Chesapeake fleet.

Setsuko and Nariko escorted Tanaki onto the boat containing Ebisu, and Setsuko directed the skipper to get underway. The boat backed out of the hangar and proceeded slowly through the Cambridge harbor, the remainder of the Yamaguchi fleet falling in behind. The flotilla emerged into the Choptank and headed for the bay. It was a bright August day, with slowly drifting cumuli in the sky, and just enough choppiness on the surface to make it interesting. The pennants flapped gaily in a winsome breeze as, for the next several hours, the vessels marked a wide circuit through the estuary at the leisurely pace of a royal procession. The god Ebisu led the way, his head jutting forward, a fishing rod in his right hand, a squirming sea bream clutched under his left arm. When the fleet anchored around noon, the combined crews joined the Yamaguchi sisters and Tanaki on the flagship for a feast, the preparation of which was supervised by the sisters in the ship's galley. It was terribly festive with the breeze ruffling the pennants, the colorful seafood, warm sake, sun-burnt companions, and a karaoke contest in which Tanaki was persuaded to belt out a hammy rendition of *Feelings*.

Before directing her fleet to get underway Setsuko climbed to the bridge and addressed her employees, reminding them of the purpose of the day's festivities: an expression of gratitude for the bounty of the sea, upon which everyone associated with

Yamaguchi Enterprises depended for their livelihood. Then she removed a roll of FAX paper from the back pocket of her jeans and said: "I also have a message from our father I'd like to read." She unrolled the paper. "I offer my greetings and wish you good cheer on the day of your sea festival," she began. "And I offer my humble gratitude to the *kami* for all they have done for me and for our company. It has been over thirty years since I founded Yamaguchi Enterprises, with only one boat and the dream to provide my fellow human beings with nourishment from the sea. Japan was still suffering from the effects of the tragic war, but I knew that the *kami* would not fail to provide for our needs if we worked with pure hearts. And now I am amazed at what has been accomplished. Our fleet of ocean-going vessels is one of the world's largest, and when I visit Tsukiji, our great fish market here in Tokyo, it makes me happy to see so many buyers crowded around our auctioneer as he chants out all the seafood we offer. I am proud of everyone who makes this possible, and I feel a special affection for our employees at the Chesapeake branch, who work so hard with my two daughters. They say you have taken the words of our credo to heart: sharing both good times and bad, we will cooperate, and not forget to encourage one another."

Setsuko stuck the paper under her arm and said, "Let's give ourselves a big hand." She clapped at her employees while they cheered and hooted. After a moment she withdrew the paper and continued reading.

"There is a shrine at Tsukiji where priests offer prayers to console the souls of the fish who have offered their lives. Unfortunately, many of our fellow humans, even my own countrymen, are not taking good care of the life of the seas. I am afraid that if this continues we will be in for a very painful rectification. That is why Yamaguchi Enterprises does not engage in fishing practices that endanger the survival of any species, and you have my promise that we will never change our policy. I will continue to work with our foundation to bring better regulation to the fishing industry.

"Father closes: Today I hope you enjoy the beauty of the sea, and feel the blessings of its bounty. Sincerely, Masuo Yamaguchi."

There was a cheer for the venerable founder, then the crews dispersed to their various boats and continued their procession through the bay. In late afternoon the colorful flotilla chugged up the Choptank toward Cambridge. The expansive summer light was softening, and the god Ebisu seemed just as jubilant to be returning home as he'd been to venture forth. After returning the god to his customary place, where he'd remain until another year of seasons had passed across the face of the bay, the employees of Yamaguchi Enterprises dispersed. The Yamaguchi sisters and Tanaki walked up Talbot Street, weary from a day in the sun, but feeling a fullness that only wished to be expended in some noble and generous action.

Tanaki felt right at home as he sat on a tatami in the room that glowed of sunsets. He could hear the crackle of grilling flesh and smell a melange of aromas, a mixture of seaweed and brine, fish and sesame oil, and the charring juices that dripped from the cooking flesh. Intermingling with it all were the scents of the women's perfumes.

He reflected on the evenings he'd spent with them during the spring and summer; walking around the neighborhood or down to the river to watch the swans; sitting on the porch; or retiring to the backyard where someone long ago established an intimate garden with statues and stone benches, a fountain that no longer worked, and a trellis covered with unruly roses whose scarlet petals littered the flagging. He remembered the O-bon festival, watching the toro lanterns float into the river, and the sisters in their kimonos.

Surrounded by the aromas of cooking food, he also recalled a couple of memorable meals. One evening they'd served carp.

"We hope you like it," Setsuko had said. "It was Nariko's idea."

Nariko blushed. Tanaki glanced at her, deciding she looked more vulnerable than ever.

"It's sort of . . . for Boys' Day," she said into her plate as she clamped a clump of noodles in her chopsticks.

"Boys' Day?"

Setsuko stepped in to explain, as usual. "Of course we realize you're not a boy, but Nariko was concerned that since you never had a boys day, it might be good for you."

Nariko seemed to shrink into herself. Setsuko continued, "You've never had one, have you?"

He assured them he'd never heard of the rite.

"You've never seen photographs?" she asked. "These colorful tubes like big fish that everyone hangs on power lines and roofs?"

"When you look up at the blue sky," Nariko added, "it's like the sea, full of fish . . . swimming in the wind." The girls held their arms overhead, swaying and swimming back and forth, being the fish.

"Only the carp could fight past the rapids," Nariko said.

"Only the carp," Setsuko continued, "had the determination to make it upstream, to be transformed into a dragon." Now the girls transformed themselves, making ferocious dragon faces and noises. Tanaki scowled and snorted back at them until they all collapsed in laughter.

"I'm afraid it's late for boys day," Setsuko said as she reached for her sake cup, "since it should be celebrated on the third of March. But I imagine this will do."

"What about girls?" Tanaki asked.

"Dolls' Day," Setsuko said. "We had to set up these special dolls in front of the family altar, then fix dinner for everyone."

"And peach blossoms . . ." Nariko began, "symbols of—" the two women looked at each other, holding back laughter, then completed the thought in unison—"grace and gentleness."

When they finished laughing Nariko said as an afterthought, "We liked Boys' Day better."


On another occasion clams and abalone had been on the menu.

"Clams," Setsuko had said pertly as she placed several on Tanaki's plate, "the symbol of union."

Tanaki looked at the mollusks, watery and soft in their half-opened shells, and suddenly understood. "Ah—two joined shells."

"Exactly," she replied as she lowered herself onto her tatami. "We serve them at weddings in Japan."

Nariko spooned several of the abalone onto his plate, their shells rattling against the china. "These are symbols of . . ."

" . . .unrequited love," Setsuko provided matter-of-factly.

"Of course," Tanaki replied, picking up one of the large snails to examine it, "one shell."

"They used to give them as offerings to the *kami*," Nariko added. "The meat was cut in strips and dried and attached to the gifts at shrines. Now we use folded strips of paper instead. I guess they're cheaper."

"So," Tanaki proffered, "it's the symbol of unrequited love you offer to the *kami*?"


On the evening of the Sea Festival eel was on the menu. Fatigued from the day's outing in the sun, Tanaki had reclined on his elbows when Setsuko and Nariko followed one another out of the kitchen carrying trays packed with steaming dishes. He pulled himself up and commented on the delicious aroma that accompanied the meal into the room.

"Eel for the ox days," Setsuko announced ceremoniously, as

she lowered the first tray onto the table in the middle of the room.

"It helps to stand the heat." Nariko said.

"I hope you don't mind eating it," Setsuko teased coyly. "We know you're very fond of them."

"Let's see," he said, picking through the dish with a chopstick. "This doesn't seem to be one of my personal friends."

"We were going to prepare it *kabayaki* style," Setsuko added. "But we decided an *unadon* would be more informal—though Nariko's always disappointed when she can't break out the lacquered boxes."

On the table were three large bowls filled with jagged chunks of eel filet half-submersed in a cloudy broth. The sisters had steamed the locally caught fish the evening before, then cut them into long filets—*steaming removes the oils and makes them more tender*—and basted them with soy sauce and sweet rice wine while Tanaki listened to them crackling under the grill from the living room. Three smaller bowls contained a soup of eel liver, soy, burdock root and cooked egg.

As Tanaki carefully dismembered his eel he couldn't help but picture a more fortunate specimen, alive and free; biding its time in some quiet corner of the estuary; already knowing this would be its last season around the bay; feeling its body changing, its eyes bulging, its skin undergoing a brilliant alteration: a still undiscovered creature to whom Tanaki had already attached the most extravagant dreams of adventure and glory!

Setsuko interrupted his reverie. "You know the *unadon* style was invented at the Floating World. That's what they say anyway." She fixed her gaze on a darkening window. "You know, all those Edo merchants of the sixteenth century. Such an interesting departure—from Buddhist renunciation to wine, women and song."

"*Ukiyo*," Nariko provided, evoking the power of the original term.

"Yes," Setsuko added enthusiastically. "A world, not solid and anchored, but floating. Always changing. Sad and without permanence." Then, looking at Nariko with an amused smile, "That was the traditional Buddhist concept anyway."

"But—"

"The Edo merchants looked at it, oh, I guess, a little differently."

"Sumo, geishas, Kabuki . . ."

"Right. They figured, hey, if this world is floating, if it's all going to pass, we'd better party while we can!"

The sisters laughed as Nariko filled Tanaki's sake cup.

"You know," he said, lifting the cup to his lips, "Nothing ever stays the same in an ecosystem. In a way, that's what's so fascinating about it. And what about migration? It's all about movement—everything in nature's always moving. I see how transience can be sad. But it's also exhilarating. In fact, I think I prefer things that way."

"David," Setsuko replied, raising her cup in a toast, "with some luck we may make a Japanese out of you yet."

He spiraled his cup up in a twisted way, making his best clown face before downing the sake in a single gulp.

# 20

# Seabreeze, Inc.

Valerie continued her investigations into the construction site that served as setting for the most dramatic gesture of Tanaki's life. After leaving the Shore the day she secured Melanie Kersey's release, she'd stopped in Annapolis to look into "Seabreeze, Inc." in the state's incorporation records. This led to a paper trail of Byzantine complexity. Seabreeze was owned by a corporation called Tidewater Properties, which in turn was owned by Bay Enterprises, which was owned by . . . and so on. As far as she'd been able to make out, there were at least fourteen separate corporations involved in either a pyramidal or laterally inter-locking network of ownership. For days and weeks she'd sat at worn tables in dingy rooms poring over land transactions and corporate statements, trying to unravel a conundrum she'd decided couldn't be allowed to exist in the same universe as her-self, in the same universe as the law school with all the sensible weight of *stare decisus* behind it, with the beach, with the bay.

She phoned Tanaki over the Labor Day weekend. "Some-thing very strange is going on out there," she said. "There's an effort underway to buy up property along the lower Shore. I still haven't gotten to the bottom of it, it's so complicated."

"Who's buying it?"

"It's hard to tell. There are a bunch of separate corporations involved, but they're all related—probably just fronts for the same enterprise. Whoever it is, they've been very thorough about throwing up a smoke screen around their activities."

"I don't get it," he asked. "What are they trying to hide?"

"Normally when you find this kind of clandestine land acquisition going on," she said, "it's a sign that a buyer wants to obtain a large tract, unbroken—without driving up prices by letting on that a corporation with deep pockets is interested. They break into separate enterprises and buy one parcel at a time, keeping everything hush-hush. It's a fairly common practice, but what bothers me about this one is why would anyone be interested in that land, since the legislature has placed a moratorium on development down there?"

This legal puzzle ran along very different lines than those by which Tanaki customarily sorted out the world. "It sounds funny," he said, "but what does it add up to?"

"I'm not sure. I've got a friend who works at the statehouse. I'll see what I can find out."

"Okay."

"When I'm clear of all this," she said, "maybe we can get together. Have a chance to talk about some other stuff."

Tanaki agreed and signed off, wondering what the other stuff might be. Was she thinking about coming around again? He tried to lose himself in that pleasant thought but disturbing reflections kept crowding into his mind. Corporations gobbling up property along the lower shores of the bay, exactly where Folker had been messing with his research. This reminded him that he'd yet to confront the director with the staff's grievances as he'd promised to do at the canteen meeting—Folker had been away, then Tanaki had gotten busy on the water, then the more he'd thought about it, the more he'd questioned the wisdom of playing the heavy for the staff. Why had none of them volunteered? They were interested, no doubt, in something he'd failed to take into account—self-preservation. What if Folker up and terminated his fellowship? Anything was possible.

Yet Valerie's news was working its way ever deeper into his mind. Though he didn't comprehend it all, he sensed that something wrong was happening, and that something had to be done to stop it, whatever *it* was. Ferreting out some hard facts seemed the first step; and he had a hunch that his problems with Folker weren't unrelated, that Folker might well hold the key to the riddle.

He spent the rest of the holiday weekend doing household chores, idling, and turning over in his mind the idea of confronting Folker. As he stood beside Reynolds in the Center's shop on Tuesday morning, silently examining the latest alterations to the tracking gear, he still hadn't decided what to do.

"Something's bothering you."

Tanaki didn't reply, fearing that merely to speak would start the slide down that slippery slope.

"You may as well get it out, or it's gonna eat you alive, just like one of our eel friends gulping down some soft-shell crab."

Instead of responding, Tanaki excused himself and went to the canteen, where he sat for half an hour trying to talk himself out of what he was about to do. He reviewed his career in his mind—the years of college and graduate school, his doctoral research in Europe, the stint in India, freezing in northern Alaska. He thought of his grand plan to follow the eel and the rest of his research. Realizing he was about to place all of that at risk, he agonized until he couldn't stand it anymore, couldn't stand as much as one more moment on the horns of this particular dilemma.

He burst into Folker's office and began speaking without greeting him.

"Guy, there are a number of us on the staff who'd like to know what's going on around here." He was breathing funny and his face was growing flushed. Like most people who avoid confrontations, he was little practiced in the art of conducting them elegantly.

"What do you mean, Dave? Please sit down."

Tanaki didn't move. "We'd like to know what's going on with all these restrictions on our research. Go here, don't go there. My plan for the season is seriously compromised. And I'm not alone." Though he knew it wasn't for the best, his voice was rising.

"Dave, please, you're getting excited. Come on, sit down."

He took a seat in the leatherette chair facing Folker's desk, inwardly vowing not to leave without an answer. "Listen Guy," he said, "there's something strange going on"—he heard himself echoing Valerie's words—"I know it. I'm sure you do too."

He noted a crack in Folker's composure, an awkward hesitation before answering. "Dave, there are things it's not important for you to know. They're administrative matters, boring stuff. That's why I'm here. To take care of that kind of business so you guys have your hands free to do the science. That's what you want, isn't it?"

"I want to go to the lower bay and finish my work in those salt grass meadows."

Folker swiveled around to face a window that looked out on the bay. He seemed at a loss for words.

"Who's buying up all that land down there?" Tanaki shot at him.

Folker's chair spun back around. "Dave," he said, his voice tremulous, "I don't know how to tell you this, but you're treading on sensitive ground here, very sensitive. And if I were you, I'd try to get along. There are bigger players than you—bigger than me—in this game."

Tanaki looked at him in stunned silence.

"Listen, I don't know about you, but I've got a mortgage and a wife and kids, and I care about my job. This isn't my research center—and it isn't yours. We're hired to do a job. I follow orders from the folks who sign my paycheck. I'd advise you to do the same."

The tremor in Folker's voice was gone. His face was growing red, his attitude hardening. Tanaki sensed that he wouldn't get any further with him.

"So that's it," he said as he rose to go. "You're taking orders from the folks who sign your paycheck?"

"I'd advise you to do the same."

Tanaki walked out, not bothering to close the door behind him.

# 21

# Chirp!

When Tanaki arrived at Moeller's lab the light was already fading around the spires of Cologne's ruined cathedral. He hurriedly parked the station's jeep in the graveled space in front, and moved at a jog toward the door of the nineteenth century mansion of brick and stone that Moeller had converted into one of the premier centers of avian research in the world. A breeze laden with moisture was blowing out of the sky to the north-east with a force that told Tanaki the season would soon be changing. The wind struck his face and with it a fugitive thought crossed his mind: hordes of Swedish starlings would soon be heading this way.

He banged the ornate knocker and stepped back, shifting restlessly on the flagging before the entrance. He was prepar-ing to knock again when the door glided open to reveal a weary Moeller. The normally impeccably groomed scientist needed a shave. The knot of his tie had been loosened. His collar was unbuttoned and his jacket rumpled as if he'd slept in his clothes. A few strands of thinning hair fell across his forehead.

The foyer was dark and the hushed establishment possessed a funereal air. Tanaki silently followed Moeller along the hallway leading to the research labs. "She will eat nothing but bird seed," Moeller said quietly, sounding as horrified as if he'd said, "she has become a vampire." As they advanced toward the laboratory

Tanaki heard the same erratic chirping he'd heard over the telephone. Moeller opened the door and stepped aside, looking neither at Tanaki nor at a large cage that stood nearby, as if by doing so he could step out of the predicament he found himself in.

Evening was falling fast, the hour when *Zugenruhe*—migratory fidgets— reaches its peak. Tanaki watched as the Bluebird hopped wildly about the *Zugenruhe* cage, the dimensions of which allowed her only limited latitude for movement. She repeatedly threw herself against the sides of the enclosure as her strident chirpings grew in pitch and intensity. He rushed to the side of the cage.

"Alright, Bluebird," he shouted over the chirps, "we get it. The joke's over."

She appeared to take no notice of him.

"Bluebird, come on. You're making me a little nervous now. Besides, Dietrich's not used to these kinds of gags. Give it up."

She stopped hopping long enough to turn and peer into Tanaki's eyes with the same wildness of the day of the waxwing invasion, that pool of inarticulate infinity, and emitted an especially loud chirp. She was wearing a yellow knit dress and she'd done something awful to her hair. It had been cut almost entirely off. What remained stood straight out in little tufts. She possessed the awkward appearance of an unfledged nestling.

Tanaki's concern was mutating into a pervading fear. He looked at Moeller, who was slumped against the wall, still unable to look in the direction of the cage. He'd been right. This was no joke—something was terribly wrong with the Bluebird. Tanaki felt a need to do something, anything to bring back the old Ana, the Bluebird he knew, even with her kookiness and moodiness. But she seemed so unreachable, so alien. And his will was beset by horrible misgivings. Perhaps, he suddenly thought, he was complicit in all this. Wasn't it he who'd rushed to pick her up on the day of the waxwing invasion? Hadn't he driven her to remote locations so she could try to navigate her way back? Hadn't they compared one another to beluga whales and blackpoll warblers? Hadn't he called her "Bluebird"?

Unable to face his reflections alone, he floated, as if in a dream, to where Moeller was leaning against the wall. He asked him how long it had been going on.

"About a week or so."

"Why didn't you call sooner?"

"I didn't want to trouble you. I hoped it might go away."

Tanaki felt more unhappy at that moment than he'd ever remembered feeling, afflicted by a pain so intense he thought he'd cease to exist were it not eradicated. He stormed over to the *Zugenruhe* cage and shook it frantically.

"Bluebird!" he shouted, "Bluebird!" She appeared not to notice him.

He leaned against the metal of the cage, exhausted with emotion. Finally he pleaded quietly, "Ana . . ." then paused and said it again, "Ana . . ."

And whether it was because the restless time of twilight was passing (the windows of the lab were now rectangles of violet darkness) or had to do with the subdued tone of his voice or the evocation of her real name, the Bluebird calmed down. She quit hopping and came to stand in front of Tanaki, gazing at him through the wire of the cage. He would have expected her to speak now in the most normal fashion, except for the hair and that look in her eyes—that look in her eyes!

She stood with her arms hanging loosely at her sides and said, "Chirp!"

Tanaki didn't have the power to respond. He looked at her sadly.

## 22

# Bay World

The morning after confronting Folker, Tanaki handed Cynthia a request for one of the station's boats, his destination marked "Elk Neck and other sites in the upper estuary." In doing so he had no particular plan in mind. He'd assumed that facing the director, after such an agonizing internal struggle, would yield the answers he was looking for; instead he was left with a greater sense of mystification. Something now told him that the answers, if they were to be had, were out there, out in the bay.

While he waited for a reply he looked up Mark DeForrest, whom he found in one of the larger labs, straining something through a stream of water gushing through an intake pipe.

"What's up Mark?"

"Hey!" DeForrest responded, looking up with surprise. "Just collecting data for one of my studies. What can I do you for?"

"I talked to Folker yesterday."

"Really. What about?"

"You know," Tanaki said, "the meeting we all had."

"Oh," DeForrest replied, turning from his work, taking Tanaki by the elbow and walking a few yards from the basin. "I didn't think you were going to follow through." There was a remote quality to his voice, as if his interest were purely academic.

"Maybe I should report to Beth. Do you know where she is?"

"Oh, you didn't hear? She's not around anymore."

"Not around anymore?"

"Apparently Folker needed someone to represent the Center on this international exchange. Looks like she'll be in Madagascar through the winter."

"Madagascar? It seems awfully sudden."

"I'll say. Barely had time to pack."

Tanaki contemplated the streaming water. "I wonder how she felt about leaving her research?"

"I don't guess she liked it. But she didn't have much choice." DeForrest made moves to return to his work.

"Listen Mark," Tanaki said, "I didn't learn much from Folker. Says he's taking orders from the people who sign his checks. Says he's got a mortgage and kids and all that."

"I can relate to that, I've got 'em myself." DeForrest walked toward the basin. Tanaki followed. "But Mark," he said, "where do we go from here?" He strained to be heard over the rushing water.

DeForrest turned and faced him. "I'm not sure, partner. Beth was spearheading this thing, you know. Now it looks like she'll be out of commission for awhile. As for myself, I'm pretty jammed up with this study. Maybe we ought to let it drop for the time being. What say we talk again in a few weeks?"

After shoving off from the station's dock, Tanaki asked Reynolds to make directly for the opposite shore, and when they were well past the channel, beyond the point at which a possibly observing Folker would be able to distinguish the cruiser from other boats cutting along the skin of the bay, he asked him to rudder hard and make for the lower estuary.

"Okay Dave," was Reynold's only response, though his smile betrayed a certain pleasure in the unexpected decision.

As the cruiser made for south the traffic thinned out and the breeze picked up. There was an astringent bite to the air that heightened Tanaki's senses and helped clear his head. The more oxygenated water of the lower bay was an extravagant blue; a bright September sun danced on the surface. By mid-day the gently waving spartina that fringes the eelgrass meadows below Smith Island came into view along the shore. Tanaki asked Reynolds to take the cruiser into the shoals, then helped him drop anchor and winch the dinghy into the water.

About fifty yards into the grass bed the boat's hull brushed against something. The dinghy was brought alongside a concrete footing, its bland whiteness wavering a couple of feet below the surface. Reynolds struck it with an oar to make sure it was real. The footing's edges were sharp: the concrete seemed newly poured. Struck dumb with disbelief, they paddled on through the bed, Tanaki's research plans forgotten. They encountered similar footings at regular intervals, elements of some kind of infrastructure—but for what?

They hurried back to the cruiser and spent the remainder of the day exploring down the shoreline, paddling the dinghy into one broad eelgrass bed after another, like western explorers striking out over watery prairies, and they continued to find strange evidence of construction activity lurking beneath a surface that reflected the afternoon sun like a burnished shield. They were both perplexed—and uneasy. The network of footings was clearly the work of an organization with considerable resources at its disposal. And it seemed that every effort had been made to cover any tracks left by the construction. Other than the broken, branching matrix of angular concrete, the shallows now seemed undisturbed. The sun-baked breeze soughed lazily over the grass beds as it had for eons, its whisper punctuated only by the sudden plunge of a common tern piercing the surface in pursuit of its prey. It took an immense effort of imagination for Tanaki to envision the commotion of heavy equipment, barges, and cranes that must have been required to put these foundations in place. Perhaps the underpinnings had something to do with Folker's prohibitions on working the lower bay. But why all the secrecy? And what were these drowned structures for? On the trip back to the Center Tanaki and Reynolds speculated about what they'd seen. Reynolds felt certain the military was behind it.

"Let me tell you, I've seen how these boys work. People used for experiments, like guinea pigs, and never even *knew* it. Put 'em on LSD and stuff, then watch 'em go out of their minds, just for grins. And dropping bombs on whole islands in the Pacific. Didn't ask anyone's permission. No sir . . . and let me tell you something else. It might be a lot safer for us if we never saw what we just saw, know what I mean?"

Rattled by Reynolds' speculations, Tanaki waited until he got home to phone Valerie: he hadn't dared call from the station. "I've got to talk to you," he said when she answered. "It's about the bay."

"I'm glad you called. I've got some news for you, too." There was a long moment of silence.

"I'd rather not discuss it on the phone."

"Me neither."

"I know this sounds strange," Tanaki said, "but I'm feeling paranoid over here. Can we meet on your side?"

He sensed her thinking. "It may not be much better over here," she said, "but alright. I'll have Ben meet us."

"Who's that?"

"He's that friend of mine in government."

Valerie sensed wariness in his silence. "Don't worry. He's trustworthy, I know him well."

"How well?" he wanted to ask, but he knew it would sound foolish.

The pancake house, right off the highway between Annapolis and Washington, was built like a Dutch windmill, gaily painted blue and white with big wooden blades that sat rigidly defiant of wind and breeze. When Tanaki entered, feeling an irresistible nostalgia for his years in the Netherlands, he found Valerie at a sunny table with a robustly built man with sleekly styled blonde hair and the square-jawed good looks of Clark Kent. Out the window the windmill's blades partially obscured the traffic hurtling along the highway. He sat down saying, "This seems fairly secluded."

"It's not bad," Superman said, taking a careful look around, "but you never know who might be listening." Valerie spoke up, establishing an air of conviviality. "David, this is my friend Ben."

"Pleased to meet you," Ben offered, rising to give Tanaki an iron-gripped handshake across the table. He sat down and smiled questioningly at Valerie. No one seemed to know how to start—or want to. Finally Valerie spoke, *sotto voce*. "David, you won't believe what I'm about to tell you." She looked at Ben, whether for verification or support it wasn't clear.

"Something's definitely wrong in Denmark," he said.

"I've got a shocker for you, too, I think," Tanaki replied.

Valerie pulled a manila folder out of the briefcase that sat beside her chair and laid it on the table. It contained a stack of paper two inches thick. "This," she said, gesturing to the folder, "is what I've had to go through just to figure out who really owned that piece of land where they arrested you."

"Amazing, isn't it?" Ben said with the amused resignation of a seasoned bureaucratic infighter.

"Well," Tanaki asked, "who does own it?"

Valerie spoke in a forced whisper. "The same slimeballs who now own just about the entire lower portion of the Eastern Shore, that's who."

Tanaki hastened to describe the odd structures he and Reynolds had discovered in the eelgrass beds. Valerie shot an alarmed glance at Ben. "Bastards!" she exclaimed under her breath.

"Not too surprising, unfortunately."

A waitress brought their food, and Ben looked approvingly over the dishes as she laid them around the table. "Looks like the fat's in the fire," he said. He sipped from his orange juice, then put cream in his coffee and stirred it.

"Wait a minute," Tanaki interjected. "I'm in the dark here. How about giving me some background?"

"Ben's on the staff of one of the state's most powerful pols," Valerie said.

"Look," Ben said, "land use isn't my area. But because of where I'm situated, I . . . hear things."

"Like what?" Tanaki asked.

Ben spoke casually as he buttered his toast. "Like there's a corporation called Global Enterprises that bankrolls the campaigns of some key players in the government." He settled in and addressed himself to his bacon and eggs.

"David," Valerie said, "how does the concept "Bay World" strike you?"

"Bay what? What are you talking about?"

"I'm talking about a fun-filled family theme park twice the size of Disney World, with pavilions about the early settlers, the Indians, the oyster wars, simulated trawling, tonging for oysters in fakey creeks, swan rides, fish rides, a huge roller coaster that veers out over the bay . . . oh, I could go on and on."

"Val," Ben put in between mouthfuls, "don't forget the luxury condos, the discount super mall—that special blend of the surreal, the ostentatious, and the tacky."

"Where?" Tanaki asked.

"David . . ." Valerie began.

"Where?!" he repeated.

"I'm afraid it's obvious," Ben replied. "Those footings you found—they've made their move."

"But Valerie," Tanaki groped, "Valerie said there's legislation on the books."

"Sure there is," Ben said. "Unfortunately, that's never stopped anybody." He took up his napkin and wiped his mouth in broad strokes. "The fact is, a powerful member of the legislature told his buddies at Global he could do some kind of a fix. They were advised to go ahead with the scheme—that somehow everything would be smoothed out."

"Smoothed out?" Tanaki asked in astonishment.

"Sure. Remember, we're talking big tax revenue. That's music to a politician's ears."

"But how could they place those footings without anyone noticing?" he stammered.

"Where did you say the structures were located?"

"A few miles below Smith Island."

"Not too creative," Ben said, looking at Valerie, "but sometimes the most brilliant tactics are the most obvious. I figured something was up when one of Global's subsidiaries got the contract to do dredging work in the channel down there. Now it all makes sense . . . in the small hours they could shift their equipment into the shallows."

Tanaki felt a helpless rage. "But they'll destroy entire ecosystems! This can't be allowed to happen!"

"Remember, if anyone finds out where you've learned this, my political career is toast," Ben said to Valerie.

"Don't worry," she said, placing her hand reassuringly on his.

The three sat silently for a moment, Tanaki's attention fixed on Valerie's hand lying so comfortably across Ben's. "What about an anonymous call to the press?" Valerie mused. "We could try that," Ben replied, "but they'll concoct some story about stabilizing the shoreline or some similar horse crap. That'll buy Global enough time to get a majority in the legislature on board—and roll out their advertising campaign. They're counting on the public to back them up. When it comes right down to it, they figure people are more interested in roller coaster rides and shopping than spawning grounds for fish."

"I can't believe this," Tanaki said in exasperation.

"Maybe they're right," Valerie suggested.

"I've got to hand it to them," Ben said. "All the preparations were made in absolute secrecy, so the environmental groups haven't had a chance to mobilize. And once things are in place, they'll tie it up in court for years."

"But those footings," Tanaki whispered pleadingly, "they're there for anyone to see."

Valerie placed her free hand on Tanaki's, completing a circuit between the two men. "This may be bigger than we are."

Tanaki wanted to weep. Pulling his hand away, he got up and left the restaurant, nearly colliding with one of the windmill blades on his way to the car. As he soared over the bridge he was utterly disoriented. His mind was crowded with concepts he'd never expected to grapple with—Bay World, Global Enterprises, campaign contributions, political fixes. And what was going on with Valerie and Ben? Maybe she was following her blessed instincts. Perhaps he should learn to do the same. But that seemed trivial compared to the hideous news he'd just heard. How could some developer ravage a beautifully delicate ecosystem to create a plasticized version of reality? Who would speak for the power-less creatures of the marshes: the bottom feeders, the young of so many species that counted on the cover of the grasses as they grew to maturity? How would the shoppers and roller coaster riders feel when there were no more crabs and rockfish, a stinking brown sludge pond in place of the glittering jewel of the bay?

He returned to the Center, but only because there was no place else to go—he had little patience for work. He tried looking up DeForrest but learned that he was on the water and wasn't expected to return until evening, and he could think of no one else to unburden himself to, as Reynolds was up the Potomac with a survey team. Wanting to be alone, and especially to avoid Folker, he went to the lab where he and DeForrest had spoken the day before. It was deserted. He knocked about the drab space, uneasy with himself, turning jets on and off, splashing water in the basins. He went to the windows and looked out on the bay. The sky was clouding over, its turbid waters gray-green.

He sat down on the lip of one of the holding pens and considered whether to wait for DeForrest's return. In his restlessness he asked himself what he hoped to accomplish by sharing Global's designs on the estuary with his older colleague. DeForrest hadn't been terribly interested in his meeting with Folker, an encounter that had filled Tanaki with dread in its anticipation and frustration in its consummation. And the references to his kids and mortgage, and to the work he meant to complete before the season turned, weren't these his way of letting Tanaki know he couldn't afford to be involved in anything that went beyond a meeting or two? And then there was Delantis's sudden transfer—sounded like someone was playing hardball.

He went again to the windows. A thick overcast had settled in. The water was getting choppier. He figured DeForrest would have to return soon. But it was increasingly difficult to find a reason to wait. It seemed Bay World was becoming an intensely personal matter. After all, it was he who'd blundered into the construction site at the Nanticoke burial ground, he who confronted Folker, he who turned up the footings down in the salt grass meadows. It struck him, with a sense of inadequacy, that this was going to be his fight.

He left the Center and walked aimlessly through the streets of Benton, past the guest houses and nautical gift shops of the main drag, then into side streets past clotheslines in backyards, where children too young for school rode ludicrously small cycles in wobbly circles in the middle of deserted streets. There seemed no place for him. He couldn't bear going back to the lab, and there was nothing at home but the silence of his apartment—the Yamaguchis would certainly be at work. He felt vulnerable and strangely aggressive at the same time.

He found himself driving eastward on the main highway, toward Salisbury. When he pulled up in front of the squat buildings across the railroad tracks he noted the dry leaves of the locusts rustling in the gathering wind. He climbed the stairs devoid of thought. He knocked, then leaned against the doorjamb, letting his shoulder support his weight.

Morning Moon sounded far away through the door. "Who is it?"

"David Tanaki."

"WHO?"

"TANAKI."

She opened the door and looked at him with pity in her eyes. He extended his arms like a supplicant. She moved to his embrace.

He sat cross-legged on her bed, immersed in an aura of richly colored rugs and tapestries, baptized in the earthy warmth of her skin and the forest-scent of her hair. He was explaining, in as measured terms as he could muster, what he'd learned at the meeting with Ben. Morning Moon was moving about the room, preparing to leave for her waitressing job at an Ocean City restaurant. After looking in the mirror and attaching hanging earrings she came to the bed and sat beside him. She leaned against him. "So what are you going to do?"

"I don't know, but I feel like somebody's got to do something."

She pulled a small leather pouch from her jeans pocket. "You know," she said, "you're crazy, but you might have the makings of a warrior. There's something I want to give you, but you've got to promise you'll wear it every minute until this thing is over."

"What is it?"

She opened the pouch and removed a shiny black stone with indecipherable markings, and a small hole near one edge. "It's a power stone. It'll keep you safe." Tanaki's face betrayed skepticism. "You don't have to believe it, dummy," she said. "Just wear it."

She took a thin leather thong from her nightstand and threaded it carefully through the hole in the stone. Then she raised her arms and placed the thong around Tanaki's neck. "Promise," she said.

Tanaki didn't know about the stone, but he felt overwhelmed by Morning Moon's nurturing spirit. "Okay, I promise," he said, bowing his head for reasons he couldn't understand.

They emerged from Melanie's building into the late afternoon. It had stormed while Tanaki was inside, and though the earth was wet with rain, the now placid sky was broken only by floating bands of cirri. On the way back to Cambridge he stopped at the refuge, where he sat looking over the marshes for an hour. When he arrived home his apartment seemed lonely. He was free of the panic he'd felt earlier, but without any focus for the new energies he sensed budding within him. He looked out the bedroom window into the backyard and noticed Nariko sitting on a bench in the garden with the defunct fountain. He descended the creaking staircase and walked around to the back. He greeted her and sat on another bench.

"What's up?" Nariko asked.

"Things are a bit of a mess."

"Do you want to talk about it?"

"I don't know where to begin."

"Anywhere . . ." she said.

"Well, it's something involving my work, even bigger than that really, as big as the Chesapeake."

"Wow. Not something good?"

"No, something too bad to believe—some mega conglomerate's trying to take over the bay, and this guy Ben thinks there's no way to stop it."

"Take over the bay? I can't believe."

"And my boss at the Center . . . he may be mixed up in it. Damn," he said, casting bits of twig aimlessly at the ground, "I feel so frustrated."

"The boss man mixed up in it?"

Tanaki explained the situation in detail. Nariko listened with interest, then asked, "Why not fight?"

"But how?"

She responded with upturned hands.

"This thing may be impossible to stop," Tanaki said. "I have no idea what to do. And if I do something stupid, and it all backfires, it could demolish my career."

She waited discreetly before asking, "What's more important, your career or the bay?"

He didn't answer.

"Remember pure action?" she ventured. "Maybe you're having what-might-happen thoughts, and you're blocked."

"I'm blocked, that's for sure," he said, looking through the trees that stood in the yards of his and the neighboring houses. "Aargh! The cards just seem stacked against us."

Nariko picked up a petal that had fallen onto the bench from the rose arbor. She held it between thumb and forefinger, turning it over as it caught the light from different angles. She held it toward Tanaki, then released it to the breeze that gaily played through the yard.

# 23

# *The eel II*

Tanaki rose after a night of broken sleep and strange dreams. He moved uncertainly to the bathroom. He looked into the mirror and tried to recognize the man who stared back at him. The result was inconclusive. He put toothpaste on the brush and vigorously cleansed his teeth, as if he could so easily clean the confusion out of his life.

He stood in the middle of the living room, as he'd done the day he took the apartment, trying to feel some directional instinct, but nothing emerged. He called Morning Moon, thinking she might be able to help, but there was no answer.

He sat on an orange crate looking at the magnolias. Sunlight fell on the floor. Life was going on, but he felt at a loss, every impulse turning inward and finding a dead end. Sitting still became unbearable, and driven by his discomfort, he went back to the bedroom. He applied himself to dressing with an exaggerated vigor and discovered that with an immense effort he could put Bay World out of his mind. He decided, for reasons of self-preservation, that for the moment he'd concentrate on something he understood better. Something from which he could expect to derive a comforting sense of purpose. He'd devote the day to preparations for the eel study.

After overcoming Tanaki's reservations, Reynolds had assembled one of the most sophisticated telemetry systems ever used in animal tracking experiments. He'd fielded a number of attachment devices on live subjects, whom he harried around the Center's holding tanks to put the equipment under maximum stress. The transmitters and receivers were tested throughout the bay, and he and Tanaki agreed that there was a reasonable chance they'd be able to follow a spawning eel as it made its way through deep ocean to the Sargasso Sea.

Tanaki signed out a boat, and he and Reynolds headed across the bay and south to the mouth of the Patuxent. They were carrying a couple dozen wire eel traps of the most modern design, along with Joe Pasquath's antiquated wicker version. Tanaki had little confidence in the relic, but as Reynolds had taken a shine to it, he agreed to bring it along. "Now that's what I call an eel trap," Reynolds had said when Tanaki walked into the Center's maintenance shop after returning from Chicawan Creek.

They motored upstream for a couple of miles and began dropping traps, attaching plenty of line and small marking buoys before throwing each one overboard. Reynolds insisted on placing Joe Pasquath's personally, and at his insistence the boat was anchored near the mouth of a shallow creek where he waded upstream with the trap, returning empty-handed with a big smile on his face.

"That one's gonna hit. I just know it," he said as he climbed into the boat. "I just know it," he repeated, rubbing his hands with the gusto of a younger man.

Being out on the water had been good for Tanaki, but by the time he and Reynolds returned to the Center he once again found himself feeling rudderless. The stratagem of concentrating on the eel study had worked temporarily, but there was nothing further to do until it was time to check the traps in a week. He didn't mention the matter of Bay World to Reynolds, uncertain how far he should widen the circle of cognoscenti until he knew how to respond to the situation. He returned home feeling tense, and was grateful to find an invitation to dinner at the Yamagu-chis posted on his door. He figured Nariko's solicitude was behind it, but that didn't especially embarrass him, so accustomed had he become to their goodwill.

## 24

# *Blowfish*

At seven sharp he walked up to the Yamaguchis' place. Setsuko let him in, and didn't mention his discussion with Nariko, though he felt certain she knew all about it. Nariko was in the kitchen as usual, but contrary to custom, Setsuko didn't excuse herself to help with dinner. Instead she remained in the living room with Tanaki, keeping his sake topped off while they discussed the changing weather, the seasonal migration patterns of Yamaguchi Enterprises' quarry, and the upcoming local elections. He guessed that a decision had been reached not to leave him alone, and while he appreciated the sisters' concern, he began to feel that he'd worried them unduly.

"So," he asked, "why aren't you helping Nari with dinner tonight?"

"I'm not exactly, well, qualified to prepare this dish."

"Really?" Tanaki asked. "I didn't know there were qualifications for cooking dinner."

"For *fugu* there are."

Here was a Japanese word Tanaki knew, since it applied to a fish, and a rather notorious one at that. "Oh," he replied, trying not to sound alarmed, "We're having blowfish?"

"You don't mind, I hope," Setsuko said. "I know it's said that a man who's his own sushi chef has a fool for a customer, but Nari has her first class license from the Ministry of Health and

Welfare—Japanese of course. And she learned right at the top, a two-month course at Tsukiji." She turned toward the kitchen and raised her voice. "Right little sister?"

Nariko stuck her head around the corner and smiled at Tanaki.

"Don't worry, David-san," Setsuko continued. "You're not going to end up like Bando."

"Bando?"

"He was our favorite Kabuki actor."

"Was?"

"Well, yes. You see, he got a little cocky one night after a big performance. He talked this sushi chef into serving him a *fugu* liver—you know, that's where the poison is concentrated."

Nariko rounded the kitchen wall carrying a tray full of dishes.

"His last performance consisted of writhing and drooling on the floor of a sushi house. No wonder they don't let the imperial family eat the stuff, right little sister?"

Nariko set the tray on the table in the midst of the tatamis and stood very erect, a schoolgirl about to recite her lessons. "The poison is found in the liver and ovaries. One thousand times more potent than cyanide, it attacks the motor-nervous system. Within twenty minutes it overwhelms the respiratory system. There is no known antidote."

"Very good," Setsuko said. "I see you still remember your lessons."

Tanaki noticed that Nariko hadn't hesitated once during her recitation. He was also struck by Setsuko's references to her as "little sister." He couldn't recall her addressing Nariko like that in the past. He remembered their account of Dolls' Day, with dolls and peach blossoms, "symbols of grace and gentleness," and could hear their carefree laughter. But things were different tonight: their words and movements seemed studied, formalistic, some kind of *schtick*. He might have guessed they were clowning around to cheer him up, except for Setsuko's tantalizing references to the dangers of eating *fugu*, with assurances that little sister would make sure he was safe. It was like the good-cop, bad-cop routine he used to watch in all those old movies on TV. But if he were under investigation, of what crime was he suspected? Had Nariko, through some uncanny feminine intuition, sensed he'd come from the embrace of another woman when they spoke in the garden the evening before?

The Yamaguchis were arranging dishes on the table. As they sat down, Setsuko resumed the conversation.

"In fact," she said, "Nariko completed the final exam well before the rest of the class. How long did it take you? I can't remember?"

Nariko held up two fingers.

"That's right," Setsuko continued. "Two minutes." She looked at Tanaki. "Amazing, isn't it? Most of the class took the full fifteen minutes to separate the good parts from the bad. But Nari always works fast. And she hasn't gotten too sloppy—yet." She threw back her head with a hearty laugh and took a slug of sake.

Tanaki belted down a large gulp of the warm brew himself, then looked at the dish before him. On a small plate were a couple of carrot garnishes arranged around the toasted fins of the blowfish. Setsuko placed an empty bowl in the middle of the table.

"We usually start with the fins," she explained. "It's best to pour sake over them." She held a fin over the empty bowl and poured from her cup. She bit into the fin with extreme delectation. Nariko followed suit.

Tanaki nibbled tentatively and asked, "I don't get it. What's the attraction in eating something that could kill you? Isn't it like Russian roulette?"

"Well," Setsuko said. "A lot of connoisseurs say they just like the flavor, though of course there are scads of tasty fish. It's also supposed to be an aphrodisiac. I guess sex fiends go for it for that reason."

"Sex fiends!" Tanaki thought. Maybe they did know about him and Morning Moon. He took a long, slow draught of sake and began to feel incredibly lucid, or lose lucidity altogether, he wasn't sure. Hallucinatory thoughts soon infested his mind—it occurred to him that his friends the Yamaguchis might be preparing to murder him! There was always that undercurrent of attraction anyway. Maybe they considered him "theirs." They were from a different culture, he reasoned. Who knew what kinds of ideas were caroming around in their minds, even though they'd always seemed normal enough? And what a perfect set-up. They'd say it was an accident!

"Not finishing your fins?" Setsuko asked as she and Nariko gathered up the plates. "Oh well, that's the least interesting part anyway . . ." She whisked his plate away and followed Nariko into the kitchen. They returned moments later with more trays.

"Now for the sashimi," Nariko announced.

She and Setsuko arrayed the dishes on the table and sat down. Each of the diners had a plate with strips of *fugu* arranged in the shape of an animal. Setsuko's was a crane, Nariko's a sea turtle, and Tanaki's, an eel. Small bowls contained the traditional sauce of soy, daikon, chopped scallions, bitter orange and red pepper.

"We're supposed to eat this?" Tanaki asked.

"Naturally," Setsuko replied. "Though it's usually eaten in the colder months."

"Less poison," Nariko interjected as she chewed.

"But we couldn't wait that long," Setsuko resumed. "Besides, who knows where you'll be after the season ends."

Tanaki stared at the eel design, wondering what to do. Continual additions of warm sake to his body chemistry had intensified the feeling of lucidity—or its antithesis—and he felt he would soon reach the point at which it no longer mattered.

"You know," Nariko said, "it could be the floating world."

He looked at her, puzzled.

"You ask why people eat *fugu*. The floating world."

Tanaki remained bewildered.

"Perhaps she means to say," Setsuko began, pausing to look at Nariko, "that the floating nature of all of this becomes crystal clear when we're faced with the"—she gestured with her eyes toward the sashimi clasped in her raised chopsticks—"abyss. Ato-san always reminded us that we have to act even in the face of uncertainty—and that we shouldn't neglect to enjoy life's delights while doing so!" She smiled benignly at the morsel, then said, "I hope that's what you meant, little sister."

Nariko nodded and mumbled as she stuffed another mouthful into her maw.

Tanaki looked at Setsuko. She smiled at him; he could have sworn he saw her wink. He pincered a sizable portion of the eel design with his chopsticks and, not bothering with the sauce, stuffed it into his mouth.

# 25

# Disposition of Forces

Tanaki awoke the following morning with a king-sized sake hangover. He made a big pot of coffee and sat in the breakfast nook, watching sparrows play in the magnolias. As the fog dissipated he couldn't help but laugh about the events of the evening before—those Yamaguchi sisters were always full of surprises. And in the cold morning light he realized how absurd had been his paranoid, stress and sake induced musings. He felt perfectly calm now, the kind encountered in the eye of a hurricane, and he felt a new resolve. It was fueled by a gut knowledge that he couldn't stand still, nor go back to the time before he knew about Bay World, the footings in the eelgrass beds, the disturbance of the Indian graveyard. He was facing something he couldn't go over, under, or around.

After his third cup he rang Valerie to get Ben's number. He'd had a chance to think about the two of them, and figured it was none of his business how she satisfied her instincts. He couldn't help admire everything she was doing to protect the bay, and hoped they could stay friends. Besides, considering what he'd shared with Melanie things seemed to have worked out for the best. When she answered he apologized for his hasty departure from the pancake house.

"You were pretty freaked out," she said. "I hope you keep your head on straight."

"Don't worry," he said confidently, concealing his remaining doubts from himself as much as from her.

"I can give you Ben's number. But as you could probably tell he's a little skittish about all this. You know he has his own political ambitions—afraid if he gets on the bad side of the heavies he'll never be governor."

Tanaki reached Ben at the statehouse. "Sorry about the way I ran out on you guys the other day. I guess I was pretty upset."

"Don't worry about it," Ben said. "Just remember," and his voice grew hushed, "our conversation was off the record."

"Of course. But I was wondering, can I ask you a few questions?"

"I can't talk here. Here's my home number."

Tanaki spent the rest of the day working on his notes, making calculations for the eel study. He tried calling Morning Moon, but again there was no answer.

That evening he called Ben at home. There was hard rock music blaring in the background. "Sorry if I'm winded," Ben said. "I've been pumping some iron."

If his muscles get any bigger, Tanaki couldn't help thinking, he's going to have a hard time buying a shirt.

"I want to tell you," Ben continued, catching his breath, "I feel like I should have done something on this sooner. I'm so wrapped up in some other issues. This thing just didn't get on my radar screen like I wish it had. I kept hearing tidbits here and there, but until Valerie called, I hadn't put it all together."

"Do you have any details on when it's supposed to happen?"

"It looks like they plan to start before winter sets in."

"Are you sure?"

"Not absolutely, but that's what it sounds like."

"Is that all you know?"

"Look for them to come by sea, under the cover of darkness."

"By sea, under . . .?"

"I know it sounds ridiculous, but that's what it is."

"Any more details?"

"I'm afraid that's all I know. I'll let you know if I hear any-thing. I'd better not stay on much longer—good luck with everything."

Tanaki heard the click of the connection being terminated. Ben seemed like a nice enough guy. He felt sort of happy for Valerie. He wished he'd learned more, but as he sat in his stuffed chair pondering Ben's remarks, he knew he'd have to go on what-ever he had to go on, feeling suddenly certain about one thing at least: he wasn't going to let anyone spoil the bay without a fight. He sipped a cup of tea and went to bed, and fell into a sleep more profound than he'd experienced for weeks. He dreamt that he was an eel swimming freely and strong in open ocean. He passed fishes of various kinds, large and small, but they all looked like people he knew: the Bluebird, Reynolds, Valerie, Pannenburg, Morning Moon, the Yamaguchis, his parents, even his grandfa-ther. He heard a strange, ethereal music. Though he was deep under water, sunlight permeated his surroundings and he could breathe freely. He woke up feeling vital and clear. After break-fast he called Helen Conway and asked if he could come over to Easton and talk with her.

"I've been meaning to get in touch with you too," she said, as they waited for lunch in the sun-spangled courtyard of the same hotel where he'd addressed her club in the spring. She looked down and fussed with her napkin, speaking reluctantly. "I was hoping you might lead our fall migration tour."

"Well," he said, "I actually have another adventure in mind."

"Oh really? My gals and I are always ready for adventure. Tell me about it."

He described what he knew of Global's plans, and told her that he needed a cadre of allies to act as lookouts along the shores of the bay as winter drew near.

"I'm sure I speak for the club in saying we wouldn't dream of missing a chance to confront these barbarians," she said, her eyes flaring brightly. "Give me a day or two to contact everyone, then just let us know what you need."

The next day he went into the Center. He requested a boat and cruised over the bay with Reynolds to check the eel traps. Amid the privacy of the churning waters he filled him in.

"So it wasn't the military after all," Reynolds said. "I'll be damned."

"No, but I have a feeling these guys could be just as scary."

"Listen," Reynolds said, "forget about that. Main thing is don't worry. Take it from me—I've been in some struggles. When your cause is right, you do what you have to do and don't let the worries get to you. Now let's see about them eels."

Reynolds piloted the boat up the Patuxent toward the traps. As one wire device after another came up either empty, or with a specimen that displayed none of the physiological changes that would indicate an imminent spawning migration, he evinced not concern, but satisfaction. "I knew we wouldn't get anything with these traps," he said as they pulled the last of them out of the river, dripping with pungent green water and strands of soggy vegetation. "Just let me check that Indian trap. Now that's an eel trap." And sure enough, as he came tripping toward the boat through the shallows of the creek, holding the wicker contraption over his head with both hands, he hollered out, "We got one! This baby will run, I can see it!"

Tanaki agreed. Its eyes bulged out of its head and its new ocean skin gleamed iridescent through the interstices of the basketry. He was pleased. It was a large, healthy female. He judged her to be fourteen years old. In the cruiser's portable lab, Reynolds held the wriggling, writhing creature on an examination table while Tanaki measured and examined her from every conceivable angle. Finally, Reynolds tenderly fitted the transmitter at the base of the caudal fin and released her back to her home.

A few days later Tanaki spent an evening with the Yamaguchis.

"I feel funny asking for your help," he said, after updating them. "It could involve some risk for you."

"The only risk is what-might-happen," Nariko said.

"Besides," Setsuko added, "the bay has given us so much. How could we stand by and see it come to harm?"

Tanaki and Reynolds looked up Buzz Richardson at one of the usual haunts. "I'd like to help in any way I can," Buzz said directly, upon learning of the impending assault on the estuary that had nourished him and his family throughout the years.

As autumn ripened, yellow and orange, Tanaki drove to Muddy Creek, finding Bob Haskel in much the same plight as before, only worse. His house was still surrounded by the flock of snow geese the Canadian government hadn't allowed him to lead north the year before, but in addition there were scores of other geese and swans, early migrants who'd gotten wind of Haskel's largesse and decided to crash the party.

"I've got to do something—soon!" he yelled as he stood on the front lawn, surrounded by his squawking wards, the idling engine of his plane adding to the din. "But I'm hoping I can hold out until the final phase is completed."

"You mean . . ."

"Yeah, I've gotten this group pretty good at following my craft. Now to see if they can transmit their knowledge to the massive flocks that'll be showing up next month."

"But Bob, you've got several intermediate steps until you're ready for that, don't you?"

"That was my plan, good buddy," Haskel replied as he patted Tanaki on the shoulder, "but I'm of a mind to just go for it. Know what I mean?"

Tanaki, remembering that Haskel's wife was still "visiting friends," resisted the urge to remind his colleague about the need to follow protocols and schedules. Taking him by the elbow, he guided him away from the noise of the plane and filled him in on Global's plans.

"This means war," Haskel replied tersely as he strapped on his goggles and strode toward the plane.

Tanaki had decided not to let Valerie in on his plans—he was no expert on the matter, but was pretty certain that the kinds of things he had in mind wouldn't exactly pass legal muster. Toward the end of October she called him at the station.

"I'm worried about you."

Cold comfort: the solicitude of a woman who's taken a pass on you. "I'm fine."

"I'm still worried."

"Don't be. Believe me, everything's fine."

"Everything's fine? As freaked out as you were a couple of weeks ago, now everything's fine? I can't believe you just forgot this whole Bay World business. I haven't."

"I didn't figure you had. Only with your position and everything, there's no point in getting mixed up in . . ." he hesitated abruptly.

"In what?

"Nothing," he said. "It's just good to keep your nose clean."

"Nonsense. I've filed suit on behalf of Melanie's group."

"But you remember what Ben said. By the time it works its way through the courts, it'll be a done deal."

"I don't know what else can be done."

"I'm sure everything will work out fine."

"Why do you sound guarded, like you're hiding something?"

"I've just got a lot of work to do."

"David—" she said finally, afraid she was losing him.

"What?"

"Don't do anything crazy."

Meanwhile Tanaki hadn't neglected his research, regularly

evading Folker's guidelines to continue his investigations of the salt grass beds in the lower estuary. He didn't like the eerie feeling that came over him when he encountered the concrete footings, but he did his best to document the impact of the invasive structures on the living creatures who now lived in their shadows.

He kept trying to reach Morning Moon, but she didn't return his calls. He had no time to ponder the reason.

The day before Halloween he discovered in the mail a manila envelope covered with foreign postage stamps. His heart sank and rose with a sad elation as he recognized the unmistakable hand—the letters artfully rendered in green felt pen—and the Italian return address.

Over the years since the Bluebird's crack-up Tanaki had stayed informed of her situation through Moeller. After the episode with the *Zugenruhe* cage she was committed to a psychiatric hospital, where she refused to utter a human sound to anyone, including Tanaki. Though he spent many weeks at her side, at the expense of the starling study with the Swedes, when his European grant ran out he made the excruciating decision to move on with his life and career, accepting a new offer in India. Fortunately Moeller didn't abandon his protégée. He visited regularly, discussing ongoing research as if it were no matter that his companion never responded with anything beyond a strident chirp if her feelings ran averse, or a soft cooing if she agreed. Over the months even these sounds diminished, but Moeller carried on his monologues unperturbed while she stared out the window in silence. After a year of this absurdist drama she finally handed him a piece of scrap paper upon which she'd written a request to meet Perdecci. Though he wasn't sure what his former mentor would make of his peculiar fledgling, Moeller was greatly heartened that she'd returned to the world of human communication. He convinced her parents to arrange a transfer to a hospital near the old Italian's home in Milan and entreated Perdecci to intercede.

The great researcher was bound to oblige one of his favorite students, but he came away so charmed by the Bluebird's fey sadness that he soon made a regular habit of visiting. After a few months she began writing notes comprised of questions about his theories, and before a year was out he found himself engaged in lengthy discussions on migration, astounded by her insights.

Tanaki had stopped writing after a couple of years, tired of wounded anticipation and unrequited gestures, suspecting he'd become more of a bother than a support. He knew she may have felt abandoned, resentful of his leaving Europe, but from his point of view he'd had no choice. At least Moeller had kept him informed of his old friend's life. She finally left the hospital to take a position at Perdecci's university, though she hadn't made an effort toward new research. Tanaki couldn't believe her pioneering spirit could remain caged forever.

It was with trembling hands that he opened the large envelope, still standing at the row of rusty mailboxes that hung on one side of the dark foyer with its antiquated heirlooms. He felt a keen disappointment when he found, not a letter in the Bluebird's hand, but an issue of the British journal *Migration Soundings*. He walked up the stairs to his apartment, sank into his chair, and opened the journal to the table of contents. An arrow in green ink had been drawn to the last article in the issue, "Navigation by Magnetic Sensitivity in *homo sapiens sapiens*."

He hurriedly turned the pages to the back of the journal. The article described an experiment carried out by none other than his onetime Swedish collaborators. They'd fitted out a dozen men and women with headgear resembling rugby helmets—there was one grainy black and white photograph—containing powerful magnets. This faux rugby team was loaded into a windowless van and transported to a destination with which they were unfamiliar. The route involved innumerable twists and turns and covered over two hundred miles of road. At its terminus the participants were asked to point in the direction from which they'd set out. A control group was subjected to the same experience, but without the magnetized headgear. The purpose of the study, according to the abstract, was "to determine if a statistically significant number of the control group could correctly state the direction from which their journey had originated in the absence of visual cues; and if such an ability did exist, whether the wearing of magnetized headgear impaired that ability, suggesting some role in *homo sapiens sapiens* for navigation through sensitivity to the earth's magnetic force lines."

Tanaki eagerly read through the article to the end, where the authors summed up the results of the study with the following words: "Our results showed a statistically significant ability to orient to the point of origination among the control subjects, while among those wearing magnetized headgear there was no such correlation." After the printed text, like a single drop of rain on a desert flower, there was a message in the Bluebird's hand, three short words written with the green felt pen: "Be the bird." It was signed "Ana." This brief communication, the first Tanaki had had from the Bluebird since her last, fateful chirp, seemed to beg a response of some kind. But he was now at the center of a swirl of events which demanded every ounce of his attention. He'd decided to confront Global Enterprises' planned assault on the bay with every resource at his disposal. At the first sign of the conglomerate's advance guard he was prepared to set in motion a line of defense that, while lacking in sophistication, possessed the advantages of surprise and directness.

There was one problem. The pursuit of the eel, which he and Reynolds had spent so much time and effort planning, could begin at any moment. Once that eel decided to head for open ocean, nothing could change its mind. If Global moved first he could deal with them and then follow the eel. If the eel were to make its move, however, a choice would have to be made, one that Tanaki still didn't know how he would settle as the dark evenings of November came to the shore.

## 26

# Battle at Sea

It was nearly midnight. Tanaki and Reynolds leaned against a counter in the Center's maintenance shop, quietly chatting about nothing in particular. Other than the two of them the station was deserted.

They were becoming accustomed to this vigil. They'd spent every night for the last two weeks here, watching the glowing red and green LED's on a small black box, alternating naps on temporary cots, waiting for the unique combination of signals that would indicate that their eel was swimming down the Patuxent and into the bay. Overnight bags were packed and the Center's ocean-going cruiser stood at the ready with a tank full of gas.

But the two men were also alert to the possibility of another signal—the shrill chirping of the pager on Tanaki's belt that would indicate that Global Enterprises had begun moving through the estuary. Along the lower shores of the bay, ladies of the Chesapeake Avian Support League peered through the lenses of field glasses through which they normally searched treetops for flecked vireos and northern orioles, scanning the dark waters of the Virginia capes for any sign of Global's impending assault.

"Davy!" Reynolds boomed suddenly.

"What?"

"She's movin' out!"

"Are you sure?"

"No doubt about it."

Tanaki looked at the tracking receiver. A row of green lights was running through a pattern of repeated elongations. "Looks like it's decision time," he said, staring mesmerized at the display. Reynolds was taking hold of his overnight bag when Tanaki's pager started pealing aggressively, audibly mirroring the receiver's flashing lights.

"Jesus Reynolds, it's all happening at once!" Tanaki said, his voice betraying his agitation. "What are we going to do?"

The older man dropped his bag and approached Tanaki, taking him by the shoulders. "Relax. Everything's gonna work out. I'm going to get the boat ready, and you've got some calls to make." Reynolds hustled out the door of the shop, bulging at his sides with canvas bags and radio equipment.

It was dark on the water. The moon was in its first quarter and it had rained the day before—classic conditions for the onset of eel migration. A misty steam rose from the surface of the bay as the station's cruiser churned through the dark mass, heading toward the mouth of the estuary. Tanaki piloted the craft with the engine at full throttle. Reynolds sat near him on the bridge, where his receivers were arrayed in an orderly row. When they passed the mouth of the Patuxent the eel still hadn't moved from the river into the bay.

"She's just hanging there," Reynolds said. "She came down out of the creek alright, and came right down the river channel. But when she got near the bay she circled back and made a pass upstream. She's done it two or three times now."

Odd, Tanaki thought, easing up on the throttle. Was she experiencing misgivings, fearing the dark and strange journey that lay ahead? Or just indulging a moment of nostalgia for what had been home, savoring one last time the unique bouquet of scents, the particular signature of water pressure and currents, those identifying characteristics by which marine animals experience their environments? "Let's keep going," he finally said, thrusting the throttle forward. "I'm certain she'll get on her way. As long as you've got a signal I'm alright."

For half an hour they cruised steadily, suspended under the blanket of the night, each lost in his own thoughts. Suddenly the ship's radio crackled. "Yamaguchi One to Tanaki, Yamaguchi One to Tanaki. Come in."

It was Setsuko's voice. Tanaki smiled with satisfaction. She and Nariko had positioned their fleet along the shores of the bay, paying the crews overtime throughout the night to help maintain the watch. Immediately after receiving Tanaki's call from the station they'd rushed to their cigarette boat and skimmed over the surface of the bay to join the fleet. Setsuko's disembodied voice sounded relaxed and upbeat.

"I've got little sister with me and we're ready for action."

Tanaki could hear Nariko's laughter in the background.

The station's cruiser proceeded and the Yamaguchi fleet fell in behind, forming an unlikely battle group.

"Lordy," Reynolds whispered solemnly, "it's like the Pacific theatre all over again."

Tanaki looked at him anxiously. "You gonna be alright?"

"Don't worry," he responded as he tweaked dials on his receivers, "I got this sucker under control."

For another hour, Tanaki and Reynolds, followed by the Yamaguchi crews, surged over the bay, seeking their quarry. The forces of Global Enterprises first appeared like a field of stars twinkling in the mist, the distant running lights of their powered barges all that could be seen. While Tanaki backed off the throttle to stand marveling at the spectacle, Reynolds tapped his thigh and said excitedly, "Look at this!"

He gestured toward both shores. Joining the fleet were an odd assortment of old workboats: crab boats, oyster boats, even a few galloping skipjacks with their sloop-rigged sails swaying back and forth. It appeared to Tanaki there must have been more than fifty vessels. Again the radio crackled.

"Buzz to Reynolds, Buzz to Reynolds, come in Reynolds."

"Hot dog," Reynolds said to Tanaki, "it's Buzz."

By the time the watermen's boats had fallen into position, Tanaki's motley fleet was within a football field's distance of the approaching flotilla of barges. Hazy outlines of hulking structures could be distinguished through the mist. Tanaki's group was running without lights and remained undetected by the pilots of the Global forces. He asked Reynolds to raise Setsuko.

"Reynolds to Yamaguchi One, Reynolds to Yamaguchi One."

"Yes boss?" Setsuko responded cheerfully.

Reynolds handed the microphone to Tanaki. Tanaki spoke into the device while looking over the water toward the Global flotilla. "I think it's time we see what we're dealing with, don't you?"

"I absolutely agree,' Setsuko responded, and suddenly there was the jolting clank of high voltage transformers, followed by a blaze of light that flooded the bay with the garish glare of a flash camera. The Yamaguchi crews had turned the floodlights used for night fishing toward the approaching barges, and the powerful lamps mercilessly revealed an unbelievable scene.

Floating toward Tanaki's rag-tag fleet were at least twenty powered barges, each carrying a gigantic replica of some wild animal native to the bay, or an historic figure associated with the tidewater area. There was a tundra swan several stories high, a sprawling blue crab the size of the research station, even a huge oyster whose shell could open and close, allowing visitors to go inside for a tour of the animal's insides. There were equally sizable replicas of John Smith and Pocahontas, Lord Calvert, and Harriet Tubman. These gargantuan figures came swaying and staggering across the surface of the bay, dipping and lurching with the motion of the water, forlorn ghosts returning to the scenes of their long-quieted struggles.

The jig was up—the pilots of the barges now realized they weren't alone. They began a series of feints and dodges, or perhaps the engines had merely been put in reverse. Tanaki was determined not to let them off the hook easily. He directed the Yamaguchi boats to begin an encircling maneuver. The barges were slow and unwieldy, no match for Yamaguchi's sleek, modern fishing vessels. The enemy flotilla was soon surrounded.

"David-san," Setsuko's voice broke from the radio. "Request permission to reel in the catch."

Tanaki leaned back in the captain's chair and pronounced with relish, "Permission granted."

At that the fishing boats began spooling out immense runs of netting, enmeshing the teetering, fantastical forms in an unbroken web of knotted nylon. Some of the engines began to sputter. Meanwhile the watermen moved in. They approached the barge's propellers and tossed crab pots and oyster tongs into the works.

"Dave," Reynolds said, his eyes intent on the tracking receiver. "She's coming!"

"Where is she?"

"Probably not more than a tenth of a mile up-bay. She'll be passing underneath soon."

Tanaki looked out at the struggle on the water, the Yamaguchi fleet and watermen tightening their noose around Global's barges.

"What do you wanna do?" Reynolds asked.

"I'm not sure," he replied. He tried to come to a decision logically, but one phrase kept coming to the surface of his thoughts: "be the eel!"

The eel had already gravitated to the bay's deep central channel, as if eager and ready for the far greater depths of the Atlantic. She felt vigorous and strong, though she hadn't gotten used to her bulging eyes, her expanded air bladder. In the darkness of the water she sensed she was swimming past strange creatures, smelled smells she'd never encountered in the protected tributary where she'd spent her life, but she didn't stop to investigate. She was through with idle curiosity, as she was through with nostalgia and trepidation. She was a swimming machine with a destination and a job to do. If she was aware of the drama being played out on the surface as she approached the scene of battle, it was an awareness of a certain amount of meaningless noise, signifying nothing.

*Be the eel.* Tanaki allowed himself to indulge the small, silly voice, and pictured her, vigorously sidewinding under the keel of the boat, oblivious to his dilemmas. Suddenly his decision was made. The eel would continue her migration just as her ancestors had done for millions of years, regardless of what Tanaki decided to do tonight. That was her destiny. And Tanaki knew his destiny was here in the thick of the struggle he'd precipitated. After all, wasn't the struggle about the eel itself, and about trash on the beach, the bureaucratic mess at the station, Reynolds' double victory, campaign contributions and crooked politicians, Indian graves, and all the rest? And having made his decision, he found himself smiling at the thought that, for now at least, the spawning journey of *anguilla rostrata* would remain a mystery.

As he began to convey his resolve to Reynolds, his eyes were drawn, by his colleague's fixed gaze, toward the sky. He perceived the first faint and finally deafening sounds of flapping and fluttering, squawking and honking, and saw the stray aerial bodies that grew into an endless cloud of geese and swans and ducks. While a transfixed Reynolds chanted, in an emphatic whisper, "Go geese, come on geese!," a buzzing aircraft dipped into the circle of the Yamaguchi spotlights, almost indistinguishable from the riotous swarm of wheeling, shuttling birds that surrounded it. The flocks, which Tanaki estimated in the thousands, swooped down on the pilot houses of the barges and sowed rank confusion among Global's forces.

"Damn, Bob," Tanaki hooted out loud, grasping Reynolds by the arm, "you did it!"

Meanwhile, parties of watermen were coming abreast of the barges, climbing the beleaguered giants, nearly naked except for war paint, a tacit allusion to a more famous act of subversion. And Tanaki couldn't believe his eyes when he saw cutting through the choppy waves, heading directly toward the lead barge, a canoe, with Joe Pasquath paddling, and Morning Moon in fringed and medallioned buckskin, a single feather in her hair, standing proudly in the bow like some kind of exotic Valkyrie. She hurled a spear at the pilot cabin, ineffective wood against the thick metal.

It's hard to say what happened next, everything was such a confusion of light and sound. The tinder and charges that the disguised watermen affixed to the barges worked better than they'd expected, and as they retreated to their boats and backed away the entire scene erupted in a massive and noisy conflagration. Barges sank while watermen and the boats of the Yamaguchi fleet rushed in to rescue the pilots. Haskel's fowl were slowly dispersing, leaving a rain of feathers drifting through the searing blaze.

"You know," Reynolds said, "if we hustle, we might still catch the eel."

A twinge of the old lust for glory took hold of Tanaki, and he was reconsidering his decision when the blaring sirens of the marine police broke through the air. The flashing lights of their supercharged boats quickly closed the distance to the battle scene. Within moments the officers were escorting Tanaki and Reynolds off the station's cruiser.

Several miles to the south, deep in the bay's channel, the eel chugged unperturbed through the chill water toward open ocean, the transmitter attached to its caudal fin sending a signal that no one would ever receive.

# 27

# *Home?*

When Valerie appeared at Tanaki's cell her demeanor was coolly professional. "We've got to stop meeting like this," she said.

Tanaki managed a wan smile and stood up as a deputy let her into the cell. He was prepared to give her a hug, but she walked past him.

Reynolds and as many of the watermen as could be arrested by the half-dozen marine police that responded to Global's S.O.S. had been booked and released. The Yamaguchi sisters, generous supporters of the police association, were allowed to walk pending further investigation into their role in the incident. Only Tanaki was being held against a sizable bail, given his prior involvement with the criminal justice system of the county. Morning Moon and Joe had disappeared in the confusion of the moment.

"Before I forget," Valerie said, pulling an envelope from her purse, "I saw Melanie the other day. She asked me to give you this."

Tanaki was reluctant to reach out his hand.

"You don't have to be squeamish about it," she said. "It makes perfect sense."

He took the envelope.

"I know we had a hard time making a connection."

"I'd still like to think we have one," Tanaki said.

"Seems like things got in the way."

"Like Ben, I guess."

"Ben?" she asked.

"Yeah," Tanaki said. "Aren't you and him . . .?"

"Me and Ben?"

"You seemed pretty cozy at the restaurant."

"Cozy?"

"You know, hand-holding and all."

"Hand-holding? I was just trying to calm him down. He was so worried about being outed. Look," she said, turning in exasperation, "he's tried to date me, but how could I go out with a guy who cares more about his ambitions than the bay?"

"I thought . . ."

"My God," she said, "you have so much to learn about women." She paced around the cell, shaking her head in disbelief. Then she faced Tanaki with a wicked smile on her face. "I ought to leave you in here this time."

"May not be a bad idea," he said, as the reality of yet another miscalculation seeped in. "I'm starting to feel at home. And it keeps me out of trouble."

"As if that would be possible," she said, her expression softening. "In any case," she continued, her tone regaining a business-like formality, "it looks like you're going to have to go back into the cold, cruel world. They've agreed to most of our conditions."

"Most of them?"

"All charges will be dropped against everyone, including you."

"What about development on the bay?"

"They're not making any commitments," she said, then preempting his protest: "but look at this." She removed a large envelope from her briefcase, extracting several photographs. "These arrived at my office yesterday. I never heard of this guy—Haskel something. Here's the note he wrote: "these photos now in the hands of every major press organ in the region.""

Tanaki examined the images. Aerial shots of the battle on the bay, lit by the Yamaguchis' floodlights and blazing barges, dense with waterfowl, boats, and sinking gargantuans. He shuttled the photos through his hands. "Bob," he said, "you're amazing."

"These should buy the time we need to fight this through more official channels," Valerie said.

Tanaki wasn't certain, but he sensed he should trust her on this one. "So they're letting me off. I suppose they expect something in return."

"Two things. First, we don't talk to the press." She turned away as she elaborated. "I readily agreed to that, since, although they don't know it yet, this Bob fellow has beautifully taken care of publicity for us. The thing to do now is get you sprung before these things hit the front pages. When the powers that be see them, they're not likely to be accommodating . . ."

He interrupted. "That makes sense. And second?"

"Second—"

"What is it?"

A tear had formed in her eye. "Damned allergies," she said, reaching into her purse.

"But what is it?" he asked over the sniffling.

"They want you out of the state—forever!"

He put his arms around her and held her snugly, looking over her shoulder out the window. A light rain was beginning to fall. *That's going some for sheer nerve*, he thought.


Though it was sunny, a brisk autumn wind swept down the bay from the north. The skin on Tanaki's face tightened as he looked over the railing. Ignoring the signs, he'd stopped the car at the highest point—where steel cables swing between mast-like spires like hawsers left behind by a doomed race of Titanic sailors—to look down on gliding gulls, forming one plane of reality, and then below, toy boats moving soundlessly through the water. He'd spent his last days on the Shore closing out his lab, taking care of personal matters, and saying goodbyes.

He reached into his pocket and removed the note from Morning Moon. "Sorry I was so hard to reach," it read. "I didn't want you to be distracted from what you had to do. I knew you had the warrior spirit in you. Besides, I can't get mixed up with a man right now. I've got to find my sacred path, and it's something I have to do on my own. Keep the stone. Good luck. Maybe we'll meet down the road."

He contemplated the note a moment. "Good luck to you too," he whispered, then held it before him and released it to the wind. A smile spread across his face as he turned his attention back to the vista of sky and estuary that lay before him. Though he was being run out of town he couldn't manage to feel persecuted. At his last delicious dinner with the Yamaguchis Nariko had said "Now you know what we mean by pure action."

"Heck," he replied, "I hope all this pure action doesn't create problems for your business."

"The authorities are trying to make life difficult for us," Setsuko said. "But we won't let them push us around. We talked to father and he's behind us one hundred percent." She stopped to refill Tanaki's wine glass, then settled back on her tatami and, looking toward the household shrine, continued. "Besides, after all this settles, and we know the bay's safe, we'll probably go back to Japan." She looked affectionately at Nariko. "Nari wants to go home. And I feel like I've gotten my Chesapeake phase out of my system."

Tanaki felt that he, too, was ready to go home. Only he wasn't sure exactly where home was. As he looked over the bay toward its northern shoals, he pondered the question and decided that, at the very least, he felt a little closer, and that perhaps it was now inevitable he'd find it. Maybe it wasn't a place at all. He thought about bridges. Had he sought them, or fled them? Images of people he'd met on the Shore drifted through his mind. They'd all gotten him over one bridge or another. The Yamaguchis, Reynolds, Bob Haskel, Morning Moon and Joe, of course Valerie. Even Folker.

Mrs. Scofield. He suddenly remembered the beauty of her spirit, how kind she'd always been to him. It was a shame about her gephyrophobia. But the important thing is that she crossed the bridge in spite of her fears. And with that thought he felt freer than a bird. He didn't know where he was going, but he'd figure something out. He owed his parents a visit. Or maybe he'd go straight to the nearest airport and book a flight to Italy, share his adventures with an old friend.

Out the corner of his eye he saw flashing red and blue lights scaling the eastern approaches to the bridge. He walked calmly around to the driver's side of the Honda and started the engine. He felt like an important dignitary as he was escorted to the western shore by four state police cruisers with sirens screaming, which peeled off only as he reached the toll gate that stood like a *torii*, not before the bay now, but before the rest of the world.

# Bill Smith

Bill Smith is a lifelong resident of the Chesapeake region. He currently lives outside of Washington, D.C.